STOLEN MAGIC

MAYA DANIELS

Vinci Books

vinci-books.com

Published by Vinci Books Ltd in 2026

1

Copyright © Maya Daniels 2021

The author has asserted their moral right to be identified as the author of this work in accordance with the Copyright, Designs and Patents Act 1988. This work is a work of fiction. Names, characters, places and incidents are the product of the author's imagination or are used fictitiously. Any resemblance to actual persons, living or dead, places and incidents is entirely coincidental.
All rights reserved. No part of this publication may be copied, reproduced, distributed, stored in any retrieval system, or transmitted in any form or by any means, including photocopying, recording, or other electronic or mechanical methods, nor used as a source for any form of machine learning including AI datasets, without the prior written permission of the publisher.
The publisher and the author have made every effort to obtain permissions for any third party material used in this book and to comply with copyright law. Any queries in this respect should be brought to the attention of the publisher and any omissions will be corrected in future editions.
A CIP catalogue record for this book is available from the British Library.
Paperback ISBN: 9781036705862
The EU GPSR authorised representative is Logos Europe, 9 rue Nicolas Poussion, 17000 La Rochelle, France contact@logoseurope.eu

By Maya Daniels

Honor Among Thieves
Stolen Magic
Stolen Oath

Infernal Regions for the Unprepared
Black Hand
Lower World
Everlasting Fire
Place of Torment
Hellfire to Come

The Broken Halos Series
The Devil is in the Details
Speak of the devil
Encounter with the Devil
The Devil in Disguise
To Look the Devil in the Eye
Better the Devil You Know
Give a Devil his Due

Daywalker series
Investigated
Infiltrated
Instigated
Initiated

Infuriated

Ignited

Chronicles of Forbbiden Witchery

Resting Witch Face

Pitch a Witch

Witch Please

Payback is a Witch

The Necronomicon Guardian series

The Magician

The High Priestess

The Courtless Fae Series

Secret Origins

Hidden Portals Trilogy

Venus Trap

The First Secret

The Last Note

Sound

Sonata

By Maya Daniels

The Cursed Kingdom

Chapter One

Most stories about redheads were true.

Fiery spirit, temperamental, mouth that couldn't be controlled, and surely there were plenty more personality traits I didn't mention, too. I was not an exception by far, although I loved to point out—on a regular basis, too—that I was different than others. What a joke that was. The moment I felt like someone was trying to tell me what I could or couldn't do, all bets were off. Logic did come into play when I made most decisions, but attitude reared its ugly head much more often. Since I couldn't do squat about it, I accepted it as part of the norm. Char, my best friend and sorceress extraordinaire, suggested we should just jot it down to genetics and leave it at that.

Pretty sure I never agreed to anything that fast in my life.

I knew the line between confidence and arrogance was very faint, and although I wobbled on it precariously many times, I never crossed it. Yet, as many great stories went, it was bound to happen, so I readied myself for an inevitable nosedive.

No one could blame me for being anything other than prepared.

My breath formed tiny puffs of mist around my face as I tugged on the thick cord that was tied around a wide concrete column on the roof of a skyscraper in the middle of LA. The air-conditioning units were sprinkled all over the flat slab I stood on, reminding me of grumbling lumps there to keep me company at this ungodly hour. A smooth texture like silk glided over my black leather gloves, making it nearly impossible to believe the rope in my hands would hold my weight when I slid fifteen stories down with only it to stop me from falling to my inevitable doom. Normal people used the doors and elevators to gain access to the business offices in the building. Thieves, on the other hand, liked to dangle outside like ornaments in the middle of the night while praying to whoever listened not to let them plummet to their deaths—the exact same thing I was doing as I peered over the edge and watched cars resembling nothing more than glowing dots below as they streaked along the street.

The misting around my face might've fooled some that LA had finally decided to give us a break from the hellish heat, but I knew for a fact we weren't that lucky. It was my magic that had dropped the temperature to minus zero—give or take—but since that ensured I could get the job done and get out in one piece, I wouldn't complain. Much.

Checking the harness one last time, I stepped on the edge backward, and the heels of my boots stuck over it by an inch. My heartbeat drummed under my bodysuit with the spike of adrenaline until I closed my eyes and took a calming breath. Distant horns and the constant buzz of life in the city mixed with the zapping of the cord unfolding as I stepped into thin air. My stomach lurched from the drop, but I focused on the hiss of the rope clutched loosely in my hands and on my reflection in the glass windows I zoomed past.

If some of the passing humans beneath me happened to look up, my black head-to-toe attire would make me nothing more than a shadow they would dismiss as a trick of the eye. I'd tucked my fire red hair under the elastic material of the hood, and apart from my eyes staring back at me from the reflective glass, for all intents and purposes, I wasn't even there. If I knew what was good for me, I wouldn't hang like a pendulum in the first place, but I never backed down from a challenge.

And this was a challenge to be sure.

I jolted when I flipped the break that locked the rope in place and kept me swaying so high above the ground, there would be nothing left of me if I fell. The drop mixed with the moonlight and the bright lights of the city until I was dizzy, so I blinked hard and focused on the window in front of me—the first obstacle separating me from what I came here to take.

"*À sealladh.*" Magic swirled around me, and I watched as my body shimmered in the reflection of the window until I blended in with my surroundings, disappearing completely. The "out of sight" spell not known by many nowadays was my usual go-to, the ace up my sleeve that had saved my hide more times than I could count.

Arm outstretched, I pressed my palm on the glass, and the chill from the window made my skin tingle through the soft leather of the glove. After a slow breath, I stretched my senses to check the area. I didn't need any surprises jumping out at me on the other side. Apart from the thrum of magic surrounding the building—something unavoidably noticed from a mile away—there was nothing else. Not a soul stirred on the entire floor.

"*Fosgailte.*" My order for the glass to open had my palm sinking inside a rippling texture as a soft shimmer covered the entire expanse of the window.

My cheeks hurt from the wide smile under my mask. Swinging my legs forward, I passed through the glass like it wasn't even there and dropped silently inside a vast, dimly lit room. I stood still, my gaze darting around the space in search of cameras. I almost dropped my invisibility spell when nothing but smooth walls met my eyes, and the backpack I wore slid off my shoulders, stopping with a bounce at my elbows. Forehead puckering, I examined the nearly empty room for any other security. Apart from the waist-high iron safe in the middle of it, only abstract paintings sprinkled the walls on three sides. From earlier in the week, I knew the door I was staring at was not visible on the outside.

"Tick tock, tick tock." I swung the slim backpack in front of me, tilting my head as I examined my surroundings. "Tick tock said the clock."

Detaching the rope from my harness, I pushed it through a loop on the backpack and secured it before removing my fingers and allowing it to swing back through the shimmering glass. It swayed on the outside, silent and ready for when I needed it. Facing the room, I pulled the mask down, and turning my hand palm up, I brought it to my lips.

"*Nochdadh thu fhèin,*" I whispered, asking the room to show itself to me as I blew gently over my upturned wrist.

Magic churned, billowing out and covering the distance between me and the safe in a frosty blue mist. As the mist traveled, ropes of angry red magic revealed themselves, crisscrossing the space in a chaotic pattern. Not impossible to pass, but deadly if I couldn't see them. Following the magic set to slice anyone to pieces to the walls, I had to be begrugingly impressed. Abstract paintings didn't adorn the walls. No, they were sigils set as wards. My spell stuck to the red magic, coating it and disarming it at the same time, so in no time at all, I strode forward, twisting and bending around it until I reached the iron box at the far end.

"Tick tock, tick tock." Crouched in front of it, I ran my hands over the smooth texture, feeling for the door. It appeared like there wasn't one, but I knew better. After a long moment, I gave up searching and blasted my magic into the iron until, from pure pressure, it popped open with a loud hiss. "Tick tock, and then it broke."

Snickering under my breath, I swung the newly discovered door open wider and froze with my arm halfway inside the safe. A wave of unease swept through me as my glove-clad fingers hovered above a leather-bound book the size of my hand. The thick tome had no visible identifiers apart from the rune etched on the front cover, which was faded from use or from the harsh hand of time. A metal latch held the yellowed pages together, the edges crinkled and blackened like it had been saved from a fire.

My knees wobbled, and I dropped on the unforgiving floor, still staring at it with my head canted to the side. The job was to break in this room, take the contents of the safe, and deliver it to the client. As always, I never asked too many questions, only collecting my fee, half of which was due before I started and half when I delivered the goods. It paid the bills, and that's all I cared about. But whatever this book was, it made me rethink my choices like never before.

I had just decided to leave it when shuffling footsteps

reached me from outside the room. My heart skipped a beat, and the muted sound of two distinctly male voices had my head jerking in the direction of the door.

"Oh, crap."

Without a second thought, I snatched the small book and slammed the door of the safe shut with my elbow. The doorhandle turned, and I sprinted toward the window. As it cracked open, I no longer cared about the red ropes of magic, bumping my hip and shoulders off the frozen magic in my attempt to get out. A bright light flooded the room when the door swung open, a sheet of golden glare illuminating the space as well as the frozen alarm system that couldn't protect them from me.

"Hey," a man shouted as he stepped inside from the hallway, but I was already a few steps short of my escape.

Sprinting on the balls of my feet, my boots made no sound. I was cloaked in my invisibility, and there was no way this person could see me. So, as I reached the windows, I spun around to put my back to the glass, and just for the fun of it, I grinned like a fool at him. Words shot from his mouth in a steady stream he aimed at his wrist, and angry curses spit from between his teeth. At the last second, I flung my hand at the safe, forming a beautiful flower—a white Kalla—on top of it. My personal touch.

My signature.

Unlike the human equivalent known as Calla, this magical sister was different in a slightly mystical way apart from its spelling. The flower disapeared after twenty four hours like it never existed. Quite fitting, if i could say so myself.

"Catch me if you can." My raspy words jolt his head up, and his sharp gaze darted around the room, widening when it landed on the flower.

I jumped, passing through the shimmering glass just as a new string of curses came from the guy. My arm snatched the handles of the backpack, and I twisted in the air, lodging my shoulder through it. With my other hand curled around the rope, I released the brake and plummeted to the ground. "*Thig thugam,*" I called my magic back to me, solidifying the glass and releasing the alarm of the sigils, wind whistling loudly in my ears the whole time. The moment my feet touched the ground, I released the rope and sprinted to the nearest shadows.

With my heart in my throat, I leaned against the side of the building to calm my breath. Reluctantly, my eyes lowered to the small book I clutched in a white-knuckled grip. My unease doubled. I absently flicked my wrist while muttering a spell to disintegrate the rope still attached to the roof, not taking my gaze off the unassuming object. Magic thrummed from it, but it was too faint for me to examine it. Shaking off the feeling, I pulled the backpack to my chest, unzipped the top, and stashed it inside.

It was done, and I was being stupid.

What could a book do?

The sooner I delivered it, the sooner everything would be back to normal.

I was the White Kalla, after all. A ghost. What could possibly go wrong?

The wailing of sirens and blaring alarms brought the quiet night to life as I melted into the shadows.

Chapter Two

"I come bearing gifts." Char's alto followed the chiming of the bell above the door as she swooped inside my store.

The sudden noise made me jerk from behind the counter. I barely missed the register as my head popped up so I could blink owlishly at my best friend. After the disaster from the night before, I couldn't sleep, and my head had a gong going off at the softest of sounds. On top of that, the client was not answering his phone, which left me stuck with the object I couldn't wait to get rid of. Something in my groan announced my pain loud and clear to the woman sashaying her way straight at me like she was on a mission.

A line puckered between her elegant eyebrows, and her chocolate brown eyes narrowed suspiciously at me while she wound her way through the glass displays and shelving. Dressed in her standard floor-length black dress that hugged her curvy body with a cloud of equally black curls falling around her shoulders, Char gripped a tray full of large paper cups in one of her hands and a humongous tote was swinging from the bent elbow of her free arm.

"Please tell me there is coffee in those cups." Dragging my exhausted body up, I leaned on the counter and made grabby hands at her, keeping my gaze as wide and as innocent as I could make it.

Just as my fingers were about to close around one cup, the evil woman stepped back, taking it out of my reach with a scowl that twisted her pretty face, making her features harsh enough to make a demon cry. Pursing her lips, she gave me a once over—well, whatever she could see of me from across the counter—and her foot started tapping the tiled floor.

Nothing ended well when Char tapped her foot.

"Did a coyote attack you on your way home last night?" One thin eyebrow arched.

"No." My jaw clenched, the move making my headache pound even harder in my temples.

"Did you get mugged?" Her damn foot kept tapping, hammering even more nails into my brain.

"I couldn't sleep, okay?" Huffing a deep breath all the way from my toes and sending a strand of fire red hair dancing in front of my eye, I stretched my arm toward the cup tray. "Gimme."

"You look like shit." Char smiled to soften the bite of her words, but she passed me the coffee she brought with her. "It's from that new cafe around the corner. Columbian," my best friend proudly informed me as I chugged down half of the first cup, blistering my tongue in the process.

"I was planning on giving them a try." Taking a more measured sip and closing my eyes, I sighed happily. "Mmmm, I like it."

Shiny black curls bounced around her face as she shook her head at me and rounded the counter, stuffing her tote under it. While Char went through her routine to prepare for the day, I did my final sweep around the store to make sure everything was good and flipped the sign next to the door from closed to open.

Crystal Palace was my happy place. Nestled between small stores that mostly attracted tourists visiting Santa Monica Pier, my pride-and-joy store carried a lot of methaphysical merchandise, from rare crystals, to tarot card decks, to exotic incense, to handmade, magicly-charged candles. While Char was in charge of keeping track of inventory and ordering it from all around the world, the candles were lovingly handmade by yours truly.

Magic wasn't an odity, per se, at least not in the last twenty or so years. Since the mages decided it would benefit them more if they stopped hiding from humans and used their natural gifts in the open, every other supernatural faction followed suit, and through trial and error—plus a few international almost-wars—everyone learned how to coexist. While all of them did their best for appearance's sake and played house, no one blinked an eye because creatures of fiction walked this earth, but they all agreed on one thing: witches didn't have room in their carefully crafted world, and they didn't deserve to live. History proved they were not wrong in their fears, but I had a thing or two to say about it.

Just to point out, I was a born witch.

While every other magical creature, apart from the Fae, could use one type of magic inherent through their bloodlines, each of them had an affinity to one of the elements, and they perfected their gifts to the best of their ability. The magic was literally in their blood. No blood, no power. Witches were a different story altogether. While magical beings had their gift of magic, witches *were* magic.

A vessel.

My kind were practically human unless we opened ourselves to our birthright. As an open vessel, we channeled it as a whole, which made us unpredictable, too powerful, and in more ways than one, unstoppable, if we succumbed to it. The origin of magic was so strong it could erode our minds and drive us insane. In which case, we would turn psychotic and go on a killing spree. Not that I had any desire to go down that path.

I loved making candles.

The bell chimed merrily behind me when the first couple of customers walked in, chatting loudly among themselves. I recognized one of the voices as a regular who came every day just to torment me with useless questions, but there was nowhere to hide. My feet shuffled faster over the tiles as I beelined toward Char and the safety the counter provided. The top of my shoulders tickled when my hair swayed, the ends of the mussed waves grazing my bare skin.

"Oh look, it's Alaska." Jasmine, the restaurant manager from down the street, squealed at her friend. "I was hoping I'd catch you here. I wanted to ask about the black kyanite shards you had for sale last week," she told my fast retreating back.

Char was grinning like a fiend, the corners of her eyes crinkling as she enjoyed the show.

"Wow, black kyanite? Really?" Jasmine's friend, who she introduced as Michelle, gushed in her high-pitched, nasally tone, and the pounding in my temples turned into war drums calling for blood.

"Morning ladies, how are you today?" With nowhere to go, I spun to face them, plastering a too-wide smile on my face.

Both women wore strapless dresses with an obnoxious flower design that made me dizzy just looking at it. Leather cords and chains hung from their necks, a crystal dangling from each, and beaded bracelets encircled their wrists. Sparkly flipflops poked from under the hems, showing off pastel-colored pedicures. My faded jeans and forest green tank top that matched my eyes faded in comparison. I felt underdressed in my own store.

"Good thing I'm off today. I'm dying from the heat." Jasmine reached inside her boho bag and pulled out a fan that she expertly opened with a flick of her wrist and a loud snap. "Can you believe it's eighty-five degrees already? June just started, for goodness sake." There was not a bead of sweat anywhere on her skin while she fanned her face.

The air-conditioning hummed in the background.

"Crazy, I know." Inside my head I was debating if my face might cramp from the forced smile I kept firmly in place. My cheeks were already hurting. "You mentioned the kyanite. I'm afraid we are sold out for now." Their faces fell, and I cheered internally. The women were human, but I had no desire to see the powerful crystal anywhere near them.

"Oh, bummer. I was hoping to get a couple for my altar." Jasmine flicked her smooth chestnut ponytail over one tanned shoulder and pouted, her Botox lips sticking out an inch from her face. "Michelle finally answered the call of the goddess. She is my sister now—a witch." She beamed at the petite blonde with red splotches on her face.

I choked on air.

I knew from the cooling of my skin that my face had blanched. Hacking and praying I wouldn't cough out a lung, I pounded a fist on my chest while my eyes watered. The two humans took a few steps away from me, throwing wary glances my way as Char darted around the counter, brandishing a bottle of water in front of her like a sword. I hoped she could see the gratitude in my bulging eyes as I took it from her and swallowed half of it in one gulp.

"Allergies." Char smiled thinly at the humans, shooting daggers at me afterward. "They always get her this time of the year."

I nodded frantically like an idiot, my hair bouncing wildly around my face and a few drops of water were dribbling down my chin.

That was all the encouragement Jasmine, the expert *"witch,"* needed. "You should dab organic tea tree oil on your pulse points and have two cups of ginger-lavender tea each day. It does miracles, trust me."

"Never trust a person that says, 'trust me,'" I rasped and wanted to slap my forehead the same second.

Jasmine narrowed her snake eyes at me. "What?"

My mouth opened because I was sick of this New Age bullcrap and ready to put her in her place when she was literally saved by the bell. It jumped and flipped above the door, announcing the next costumer. All four of us were somewhat clustered in the middle of the store, so we all turned in the direction of the chime to see who walked in. An older gentlemen with salt and pepper hair, a neatly trimmed beard, and spectacles closed the door behind him and nervously glanced around. In a light blue button-down shirt and black slacks, he stood out like a sore thumb in my store.

He cleared his throat uncomfortably, finally spotting us gawking at him.

"Welcome to the Crystal Palace." Char snapped out of it first, her friendly grin that could charm the socks out of anyone firmly in place. "How can we help you today?" Her eyes kept dropping to the large bouquet wrapped in black velvety paper the man had clutched in his hand.

"Yes. Right, yes," he repeated nervously, glancing all over the store as his face reddened. If it wasn't my business that made him fidgety, I would've thought there were foot-long dildos and bondage paraphernalia displayed all around.

Thankfully, Jasmine and her friend walked away, ducking behind a glass display full of crystal towers tall enough to hide them from view. Their whispered murmurs created a distant buzz in the background. Fingers tightening on the bottle of water, I attempted a friendly smile for the older man. He probably wanted to buy a gift for his wife, or maybe a lady friend judging by the flowers he was strangling in his grip.

"Good morning," I rasped, my throat raw from the coughing fit.

Instead of replying, he flipped the bouquet in front of his face like a shield to hide him and mumbled while rustling the paper. It was tall enough to hide the flowers curled outward in a squiggly wave. "Here it is." He exclaimed, holding up a tiny envelope in his free hand.

Char and I looked at each other.

What a weirdo.

"Alaska McCullough?" Peeking around the flowers, he seemed so hopeful I almost laughed.

"That would be me," I told him, sympathy toward the nervous man tightening my chest. He must've seen the ad for the store and knew I made the candles on request, too. Maybe a rekindling love one for the poor guy. My mind was already spinning with ideas on how to help the older couple.

A broad smile formed additional wrinkles on his face, and he darted faster than any old man should toward me.

Thrusting the flowers in my chest, he didn't wait to see if I'd catch them. He spun on his heel and bolted out of my store like the hounds of hell were nipping at his butt.

Dread pooled in my stomach, weighing it down.

With trembling fingers, I flicked the card open, and my lungs shriveled like prunes. Two words imprinted themselves in my brain for eternity. *I know.* There was no name or signature under the accusation curdling my blood. I crumpled it so hard I had to force myself to calm so I didn't turn it into ashes while humans hovered inside the store. After I shoved it in my pocket, it was easier to sip air through my tight throat.

Lowering my hand like it belonged to someone else, I peered inside the black paper, and all the blood thickly trickling through my veins drained from my face. Char snatched my upper arm to keep me standing when my knees buckled, and even Jasmine dragged her friend to take a look at my gift. I prayed to whoever listened that my face showcased that I was shocked from the surprise and not scared out of my mind. Because the flowers were not a gift.

They were a threat.

"Allie?" Not even the nickname my best friend gave me could soothe the galloping of my heart.

"They are beautiful," Jasmine gushed, a note of envy coloring her voice.

"Yeah," I breathed through numb lips, staring unblinkingly at them.

The large bouquet of white kalla lilies glared at me accusingly.

Chapter Three

People swarmed the shop in a sea of faces and blurred bodies that blended with the displays and shelving. It helped to take my mind off things, unless I looked under the counter. The flowers were tossed in the small trash bin under the register, spilling over the rim and tipping it precariously. Ignoring them the best that I could, I dived in with unwavering focus to answer questions, offer suggestions, and even help Char put together satchels for those coming to buy her potions and talismans. My best friend kept casting worried glances my way the entire time, but I pretended not to see them. Work I could do. It was healthy, productive, and left me no time to breathe, little less finish the second cup of Columbian coffee Char brought me that morning. The cold cup was silently keeping the register company on top of the glass display.

Every time the bell chimed, my heart skipped a beat.

Cold sweat made my palms slippery, and no amount of wiping them on the fabric of my jeans helped. Around noon, the crowd dwindled, and after my third attempt to wrap a medium-sized statue of Isis, which kept tearing the wrapping paper, Char took it from me and hip-bumped me out of the way.

"We are closing for lunch," she informed me after slipping a clear crystal quartz in the bag as a way of apologizing to the pissed-off lady waiting for her Isis statue to be wrapped for twenty minutes.

I blinked numbly at my friend, but she didn't wait for my agreement or any type of reply. Swinging her tote—which was large enough to carry a baby giraffe in—over her shoulder, she linked her arm through mine and bodily dragged me out of the store. We melded with the people rushing in all directions, while I clung to Char like I might fly away and never return if I let her go. As always, she understood me better than I did and tightened her hold on my arm as she maneuvered me around groups of tourists stabbing fingers at the Ferris wheel looming over everything at the end of the Pier.

Next thing I knew, we were perched at an outside table in one of the bars we liked for their tapas. While I focused on breathing, Char ordered a number of things, even remembering crab cakes before she turned her piercing gaze on me. My throat tightened from the knowing expression on her face, and it took a few tries to swallow the lump blocking my airways.

"Okay, I'm listening." Her gaze rolled around the outdoor patio, and before I had a chance to part my lips, her finger popped up, silencing the words before they spilled from my lips.

Her hand dove into her tote while I struggled to fill my lungs with the air that tasted of the ocean and coconut oil. The distant hum of voices and honking cars thrummed around me, but despite all of it, I felt like I was drowning.

So many years I'd stayed under the radar. I'd taken jobs that required my special set of skills, most of them more difficult than the last, yet nothing like this had ever happened. Everyone knew of the White Kalla, the thief, a ghost, but no one ever connected it to Alaska, the quiet candlemaker with a simple life.

Until now.

Char retracted her hand from the never-ending abyss that was her purse, triumphantly holding up a talisman the size of my thumb. I should've known she'd be prepared for any situation. Dark wood with wood on both sides was pinched between her fingers, and it pulsed with magic as she set it between us. Her palm hovered over it for a moment while a soft golden light stretched between it and the wood. My skin prickled when Char's lips moved with whatever incantation she whispered, and the outside world melted into nothingness. Years ago, we agreed to never ask each other questions about our magics because plausible deniability was a thing we took very seriously, so I had no idea what she was doing. I still didn't dare ask, although I wanted to know more than anything.

Both our lives depended on ignorance.

"Now we can talk without anyone eavesdropping on our conversation." The happiness from using her powers washed off of her, and she peered at me in concern. "Allie, what's going on? Knowing how prickly you are when it comes to jerks, first I thought a guy screwed up and was apologizing by sending flowers. I even felt sorry for the shmuck, to be honest. But the longer I watched you, the clearer it became that this is not a guy problem."

My mouth opened and closed a few times but nothing came out. It was becoming harder and harder to breathe as I gaped like a fish out of water. I'd always been careful. I accepted or turned down jobs based on experience built on confidence, not arrogance. Many times I had snatched things in front of people's noses with them oblivious to what was happening. I'd had much closer calls than the night before when the guy that showed up was the only blip in my otherwise carefully planned mission.

Where did I go wrong?

The whole thing was easy. It was too easy, and I should've known.

A warm hand covered my icy one on top of the table, and I blinked Char into focus. My friend looked sick from worry, and I hated seeing her like that. Guilt drilled a hole in my sternum because I'd never hidden anything from her. That should've been my first red flag when I left the house last night while she thought I was going to see a guy instead of leaving on a job.

"Please, Allie. You're killing me here."

She pulled back when the waitress approached the table, bringing our drinks and a few plates filled with yummy goodness. Instead of my usual drool fest when it came to tapas food, acid burned my esophagus. I found it mildly interesting that Char was talking to the girl while I was blissfully cocooned in silence, not hearing anything while watching their lips move—not that I'd complain. There were too many voices fighting for attention inside my head, and they made me nauseous and dizzy. Unfortunately, too soon we were alone again.

"I messed up, Char." It came out in a whimpered groan.

My tone was as pathetic as I felt. Tears burned the back of my eyes. When I envisioned the worst-case scenario—someone finding out who I was—I imagined mobs of people screaming "witch" while pointing accusing fingers at me as they watched my execution. Not in a million years did

I picture being exposed as a thief who used the rarest form of magic, which would lead them to the discovery of what I truly was. For whatever reason, the latter sounded and felt worse.

"Messed up what?" I could tell she was holding her breath.

"To start with, I lied to you about where I was going last night." Her expression didn't change while she patiently waited for me to continue, but I still dropped my gaze to the table because I didn't want to see the disappointment in her eyes. "I was on a job. I could use the excuse that the client didn't want anyone hearing about it and made me swear an oath to justify lying to you. But I can't do that. I refuse to do that. It was over the phone, and it won't work on me anyway, even if it wasn't."

"I'm guessing that's not why you look like seven generations of your ancestors just crawled out of their graves." She urged me to tell her everything with a calmness that didn't betray her feelings. I hated it. I wanted her to yell, tell me off, even slap me if she felt like it. Anything but the emotionless tone she was giving me.

Words spilled from my mouth in a torrent of jumbled sentences, like I couldn't wait until I had it all out in the open. Char listened carefully, occasionally tilting her head when the corners of her eyes crinkled with suspicion or her mouth tugged down in a frown. By the time I was done, I was panting and gasping for air while she leaned back in her chair with a stunned expression on her face. Our untouched food and drinks sat silently between us.

"You are absolutely sure that the flowers came from whoever owned this book before you took it and not from someone else?" Her question gave me a pause.

Rare were the kinds of friends who found out you were

a thief and didn't even look at you different, still trusting everything they owned and everything they were with you. Rarer still are the ones like Char, who also knew you were a witch but would take that secret to their grave.

Shame flooded me.

"Well, no." A frown wrinkled my forehead as I stared at my twisting fingers. "But what are the chances that someone would deliver a ton of white Kallas not even twelve hours after I left one on top of an empty safe?" The flower signature was Char's genius idea because it reminded her of my last name. According to her, Kalla sounded similar to McCullough, and I just went along with it.

"Valid point, but we can't be sure."

"We?" I was too afraid to hope while the crumpled card burned my hip through the fabric of my jeans where it still sat in my pocket.

"Yes, *we*, you daft woman." Char squared her shoulders and gave me a sly look. "You didn't think I was going to take up knitting while you have all the fun, did you?"

The laugh that burst out of me held no humor or joy. It was full of relief and gratitude while I blinked back tears. The pesky things were trying to blind me. "Okay, we then." My smile wobbled, but she was kind enough not to mention it.

"Okay, which place did you free of their burden last night, devil woman?"

A hard lurch had my heart trying to punch a hole through my chest. "Ice Matrix CO."

Up to that point, Char had been fully relaxed while sipping on her cocktail. I had no doubt she'd already been deciding what type of memory altercation potion she would feed the poor soul. But the second I said the name of the company, a shower of the sparkling beverage she'd been swallowing sprayed from her mouth and dripped down my face, one drop stubbornly clinging to the tip of my nose.

"Well"—Primly picking the cloth napkin up, I dabbed it on my skin to clear the sticky liquid from my face—"that speaks volumes."

"You know who the owner is, right?" Char croaked before guzzling whatever was left of the cocktail in one go so she could speak without coughing.

"The largest pack of shifters in North America." My mouth twisted in a grimace. "I did my homework, Char. I'm not so dumb that I would go in blind."

"Far be it for me to call you dumb. The smart woman that you are, you also know that Dimitri Bell, aka Asshole Alpha of that very pack, was just voted—last week actually—as an exclusive member of the MPO." Even though it was stupid, I muttered his name while Char arched an eyebrow at me, but then my brain caught up with what else she had said.

"What?" It came out as a shout, and I jerked upright, forgetting about the silence talisman we had sitting on the table while craning my neck to see if anyone had heard me. "What do you mean he is a member of MPO?" I hissed at my friend, doing my best to ignore the fear flickering in her irises.

Order of Magical Powers, or as it officially states, Magicas Potestates Ordinem, to that day, had stayed enemy number one to those like me. Only the strongest of magical beings were invited to undergo trials, and very few succeeded in passing them to become members. When witches were deemed too dangerous and unfit to blend with society, it was MPO that hunted them down and killed them all. They didn't discriminate between men, women, or children. With uncanny precision, they exterminated my kind from the face of the earth. My own mother was among the deceased after she managed to hide me by the skin of her teeth.

And like an idiot, I walked into their hands of my own free will.

Chapter Four

Hands shaking, I squared my shoulders and tilted my face up until a kink developed at the back of my neck, but I still stared at the top of the tall building. I couldn't see all the way to the roof because of the sun, which made my eyes water with its glare. After jumping at every sound for a full week and hoping if I pretended it didn't happen, it'd go away, I decided it was time to investigate. The fact that my client, who generously paid for the leather book that had doomed me was nowhere to be found and wouldn't answer the phone only added to my torment. After our lunch the day I told my friend everything, Char dumped the bouquet of Kalla lilies in the outside dumpster, but not before she stomped on them while growling. I could still see them in my mind's eye, although they were long gone.

"Just breathe." Telling myself that never helped, yet I kept trying.

Two security guards manned the double glass doors that continued to slide open and closed in regular intervals. For the hundredth time, I wondered why I thought it was a good idea to come back to Ice Matrix CO. in the middle of the day, but the answer didn't magically appear. Violence was written all over the tall, bulky men dressed in black tactical pants with their same-color t-shirts while they eyed me up and down before dismissing me as if I was the dirt under their boots. Same thing I was doing to them, if I was being honest. Physically, I was no match for the two shifters who could squish me like a bug with their tree-trunk legs, but magic wise, they would be dead before they had time to blink.

My black tank top was stuck to my spine from the cold sweat I couldn't stop from coating my skin no matter how hard I tried. Unfortunately for me, although the stain couldn't be seen, the sensitive noses of the wolves manning the door could smell it from a mile away. Also, the longer I lingered in front of their building, the more suspicious they'd become. So, I plastered a forced smile on my face and hurried to enter, trusting that the glamour I placed over the two daggers strapped to my thighs would hold.

They gave me side-eyed glares as I darted through the glass double doors, but when the foyer opened in front of my eyes, I forgot all about them. Gleaming white floors stretched between me and the long, modern desk on the other side of the space. The marble was streaked with gray lines that spread through it like cobwebs, occasionally covered with thick rugs in black and white tones. Dark leather armchairs and sofas were clustered in a few places with low tables between them, and vases full of blooming flowers added a splash of color in the otherwise monochrome décor.

Above the shiny black desk covered in monitors across from me, Ice Matrix CO. was written in cursive, glaring red from the white wall like a warning. Sadly, apart from a dozen or so people walking around me with purposeful strides, the foyer of the business seemed abandoned. My hopes of going in and out without too many eyes noticing my presence died a certain death, even without the narrowed gaze aimed like a sniper at me from behind the reception desk. Reluctantly, I made eye contact with the woman, and with a fortifying sigh, I headed her way.

"Good morning." The stern expression on her narrow face, along with the unimpressed press of her mouth said that the morning was actually not good at all. "Do you have a scheduled appointment?"

"Umm, no?" My squeak turned into a question, and I wanted to punch myself for acting dumb. I cleared my throat and tried again. "I do not, but I was hoping I'd be able to talk to someone regarding the open position in your company." Belatedly, I remembered that I should smile, so I had no doubt she thought I was slow or something when, for no reason at all, I beamed at her like a TV-show hostess.

The reason I gathered enough courage to enter the viper's nest was the ad I found on their website. They were hiring a handful of people for entry-level positions, one of which was an assistant to the secretary. In what world did anyone hire an assistant for the assistant was beyond me. Ice Matrix CO. was the largest security firm that catered to the powerful and famous, from bodyguards to cyber-security systems. According to the almighty Google, I also knew that the company had been in the Bell family for generations. Nine, to be exact.

Must be nice to be rich.

"And which position might that be?" One thinly plucked eyebrow shot up like an arrow toward the gray hairline as the woman's eyes twinkled mockingly at me. It wasn't hard to tell she thought I didn't belong in the place.

Hell, even I knew I didn't belong, even without her mockery.

What are you doing here, Alaska? I wished I could answer my internal question, but all I could do was blink at the dark-eyed woman like an idiot. She'd asked me a question. Right.

"The entry position for an assistant." My middle and forefinger curled around each other while I hoped she wouldn't ask me to be more specific. There were a couple I read about on the website, but for the life of me, I couldn't remember anything about it.

"I'm sorry, those were already filled." With an indulgent smile that never reached her dark eyes, she dismissingly turned away from me.

Panic clawed inside me, making my heart work overtime while I stared at her profile. I was by no means some professional hacker or anything, but I knew enough to actually find out if they had a recording of my breaking and entering. All I needed was to get inside the building, and I could disappear until I found what I was looking for. The woman was the main obstacle between me and, quite possibly, my death sentence. There was no doubt in my mind whoever sent those flowers had some type of evidence they planned to use against me. Without any, it'd be their word against mine, and I could play dumb with the best of them. To send a bouquet with a threat meant the person had proof, regardless that I didn't see any cameras in the room.

"I saw that the position was open before I came here this morning. Are you sure I can't apply just in case they don't have the right candidate yet?" Proud that I sounded calm and collected, I leaned on the desk toward the woman. She looked like she was in her mid-fifties, but I had a feeling she was a shifter too, which could mean that she was fifty or a hundred and fifty. They didn't age like regular humans.

A muscle twitched in her jaw, and her sharp, sniper gaze swung at me like a whip. Her thin, red-painted lips were already parted to tell me to get lost, but at the last second, her dark irises jerked over my shoulder, widening for a moment. It didn't take a genius to figure out someone was standing behind me. Someone that made this vulture woman blanch as if she was staring at a living, breathing T-Rex in the middle of LA. I stiffened but didn't dare turn. Keeping my eyes glued to the woman's face to better judge the situation, I waited, a little too aware of the weight of the daggers on the outside of my thighs.

"Morning, Pura," a low, raspy voice said from right behind me.

My heart punched my ribs, and goosebumps pebbled my skin. How on earth didn't I notice whoever it was when the person was standing close enough to ruffle my air with the air passing their lips? At least the woman, Pura, according to whoever was behind me, looked the same way I felt. Shocked.

"Mr. Bell." Pura jumped from her seat like it was on fire, and the chair rolled away from her until it bumped the wall with a thud. "What a pleasant surprise to see you here."

A million questions swirled through my head. Ice Matrix CO. belonged to Dimitri Bell. Why was his receptionist surprised to see him in the building? And what kind of shitty luck did I have for the man himself to be standing behind me two minutes after I stepped foot inside his building? Was it all part of his plan? Did he send those flowers hoping I'd be stupid enough to come running right into his hands? All my instincts were screaming at me to run. Instead, I very slowly turned to face him, my back pressed on the desk so I didn't fall at his feet like an idiot. My legs were trembling without control.

My eyes locked on his piercing silver gaze, intense enough it felt like it reached all the way to my soul. A frown tugged at my forehead at the slight wrinkles around his eyes and mouth, and the streaks of silver at his temples. With shoulders wide enough to block my view from the space behind him, he was dressed in an expensive-looking dark suit with a white button-down shirt that had no tie. All the photos I'd seen of Dimitri Bell must've been from many years ago because the shifter standing in front of me looked at least ten—if not more—years older. His face also seemed rounder, and his lips thinner. I also expected him to be taller, which was dumb on its own. Why I cared how he looked or about his height was beyond idiotic.

"Hello." His charming smile loosened the panic tightening my chest.

"Hi," I answered as eloquently as ever, still staring at him.

With an amused chuckle, he turned his gaze to the woman, and I sucked in a much-needed breath. "I need to see my son, Pura. Tell him I'm on my way." Those silver irises flicked back to me. "It happens often, you know." Grinning, he flashed a perfect set of white teeth at me, while Pura's frantic mumbling in the phone receiver created a hum in my ears.

"What happens?" I asked him dumbly, my voice breaking from the drumming of my heart in my throat.

"It takes a moment for people to tell if it's me or my son they are looking at." With a quick glance at Pura, he took my elbow and spun me in the direction of the silver elevator doors to our right. "Come, I'll show you where to go for the interview." My feet automatically followed him, and I was too shocked to do anything but blink at the man.

A strong hand reached out, and he mushed the button on the wall to call the elevator, lighting it up red. Numbers glowed above the doors, too, but I was so stunned that they were blurry and too far for me to notice. It must've amused him more because he laughed.

"Pura has been with us for many years, and she is very protective, as well as set in her ways. Don't hold it against her." The doors opened with a dull ping, and he guided me inside. "We need more young people in the company." My stomach dropped when we lurched upward, but I still couldn't find it in me to say a word. "Good luck. Knock on the third door to your left."

I stumbled when he nudged me out of the elevator, and I gaped at his widening grin until the doors closed, taking him away. It took a long moment for my limbs to function and for my brain to get back online.

"Holy crap." Panting, my gaze darted around the empty hallway lined with doors on both sides. *Did Dimitri Bell's father just give me entrance to his son's building?* It'd serve that jerk right if he really was the one threatening to expose me. Unwilling to look a gift horse in the mouth, I quickly scanned the doors, locating the bathrooms at the far end of the hallway. Heart in my throat, I darted in their direction before anyone had a chance to see me and drag me out.

All I had to do was find the security office and delete whatever evidence they had against me. If any.

Dimitri Bell wouldn't know what hit him.

A smile stretched my lips.

Chapter Five

I'd like it to be known that bathrooms in office buildings should never look as good as the one I stood in, but I took full advantage of it. The shoes were the first to go as I tugged them off my feet and stashed them behind the toilet in one of the stalls. Next were the earrings dangling from my ears, in case there were metal detectors that they might trigger while I skulked around the place. My daggers were made of smooth, blessed agate, so I was confident I could walk in anywhere with them strapped on my body. It took me the longest to tie my hair in the smallest ponytail known to mankind so it didn't get in my way. The length looked great when I styled it, just brushing the top of my shoulders, but it definitely was not convenient when infiltrating a security company. With that done, I hunkered down to wait for someone to open the door so I could slink out.

It was the longest wait of my life, and I prayed Pura forgot all about me and didn't check with her coworkers to make sure I ended up in one of the offices for an interview.

When the sound of feet hurrying over the smooth floors in the hallway reached my ears, I took a deep breath and called on my spell. *"À sealladh,"* I murmured under my breath and watched my reflection disappear in the mirrors lining one wall. Back pressed next to the door, I held my breath and strained my ears to make sure there wouldn't be any surprises waiting for me outside.

The door opened so fast it banged on the opposite wall, and I flinched, plastering myself to the tiles behind me as if I was trying to meld with them. Wide-eyed, I watched the man rush toward the pissers like his ass was on fire, his fingers already fumbling with the zipper of his pants. Biting my lip, I slipped through the door before it closed because I didn't want to end up with an eyeful of sausage. Swallowing the snicker threatening to escape, I looked up and down the hallway, unsure which side to start with first. The older Mr. Bell deposited me on the fourteenth floor, so I knew I needed to go down since it stood to reason that the security offices would be on the lower levels. From what research I did on the company, the first half of their building dealt with a mixture of human and supernatural clients. Dimitri would make sure no human stepped foot on the upper part of his empire, which would cater to those with powers in case they needed his assistance with something of that nature. Different rules applied to those of us with magic, and anyone with half a brain would make sure the two stayed separate.

It was what I would do, in any case.

With my mind made up, I inched to the door with a glowing exit sign above it and a picture of a stick figure descending stairs next to it. One look over my shoulder assured me that no one would notice the door opening, so I pushed through it and closed it gently behind me. My tense shoulders relaxed as the cool air of the stairs washed over me, until I noticed the camera sitting at the corner above my head. My spell never failed me before, but the words "I know" written in an elegant scroll and scratched over the small card floated at the forefront of my mind's eye, taunting me. I pushed the gloomy thoughts away and, with a firm grip on the banister, I darted down the many stairs, taking them two or three at a time. After only a few levels, I found myself pressed to the wall, and I held my breath when a door opened, the sound of shuffling feet joining me in the quiet space.

"Hmmm, I didn't think you had it in you, darling," a woman purred, the suggestive tone of her voice thick enough to be cut with a knife.

I rolled my eyes.

Just my luck that I'd be stuck in a freaking stairway while office workers got down and dirty one floor below me. When I tell Char about it, I'd never hear the end of it, I was sure. Craning my neck, I peered down to see where the couple was, but the second voice that spoke froze me in place. I nearly swallowed my tongue.

"I told you not to come here, Angela." A thick accent colored the deep baritone, harshly rolling the r's and t's and sending my heartrate into overdrive. "What is the meaning of this?"

Personally, I didn't know Dimitri Bell, nor had his existence ever tempted me to find out more about the alpha. But it was inevitable to hear about him from everyone else around me, including my best friend. Ladies spoke of him like he was the best thing that had happened to womankind, and despite my determination to ignore the comings and goings of my world, I still knew more about him than I should. Example: the fact that he was raised by his mother in her homeland away from the American society until he was in his early twenties was not news to me. His Russian accent was something whispered under breathless sighs, which normally made me roll my eyes, but I totally understood it at that moment. With a couple of sentences, he awoke a cloud of butterflies in my belly and sent them into a frenzy until I had to grip the banister tightly to ensure I didn't jump over it to see if his physical appearance matched the voice. It was slightly raspier than his father's, and a note or two deeper, with a natural growl to it that made me shiver.

I shook my head to clear the hormonal insanity. What on earth was the mater with me?

"We had a deal, Dimitri," the woman whined, and I found myself padding down the stairs on the balls of my bare feet. It took effort not to suck in an audible breath when I stopped on the landing right above them in clear sight. Thank all the gods for invisibility spells. "If I have to do what you say, you have to suffer being introduced to those in my circle."

The woman, Angela, was one of the most beautiful beings I'd ever seen. Not in the traditional sense, according to Hollywood, but in a jaw-dropping one. Her hourglass figure was wrapped in a blood-red knee-length dress with a slit on the right side up to her hip. If it wasn't for the platinum blonde hair draped over one shoulder, I would've mistaken her for a living, breathing Jessica Rabbit. Her large boobs were ready to spill over the tight strapless dress with each breath she took, and her blue eyes sparkled in the yellow glare of the light while she pinned the man in front of her with her gaze. Full lips were pressed in a firm line, displaying her frustration, and most surprising was the fact that she was as tall as him on her high-heeled, strappy sandals.

"You have bad timing, woman," Dimitri snarled, his shoulders bunching as if he was trying very hard not to grab her by the throat.

I couldn't see his face, but that didn't stop my mind from conjuring all sorts of scenarios just by watching him from behind. His silver-gray button-down shirt was tucked into his black pants, but his suit jacket was missing. The shirt itself was rolled at the sleeves almost to his elbows, displaying impressive forearms where the muscles were corded while he clenched his fists. My eyes traveled down the expanse of his back to the narrow waist and a mouth-watering backside that the expensive-looking fabric was hugging lovingly. His pants were stretched over powerful thighs, and I found myself swallowing thickly. It took me a moment to realize he had stiffened, and he spun around to face me so quickly that I had no time to bolt back the way I had come.

My heart stopped.

Stormy silver blue eyes flicked all over the stairway, and I didn't need to guess that he was looking for me. I might be invisible, but apparently all the stories about Dimitri Bell were true. His eyes couldn't see me, but his senses picked up my presence immediately. I didn't dare move or breathe. Gaze locked on the powerful alpha, I stared like a deer caught in headlights as I waited for him to pounce and shred me to ribbons. It would serve me right for being an idiot.

"What is it?" The blonde placed a manicured hand on his forearm, her red-painted nails denting his tanned skin.

He ignored her, still intent of finding what triggered his

senses, and that gave me time to examine him. I should've been running, but his chiseled features had my feet glued to the cold floor. When I saw his father, I thought the photos on the company's website were old to feed Dimitri's ego, but it became more than clear they didn't do him justice. His square jaw was clean shaven and his harsh slash of lips twitched as he barely contained a snarl. His eyes had storms brewing above the sharp cheekbones, and my blood turned to icicles when a smile bloomed on his face, bringing to life a set of dimples.

"Nothing." Straightening, he turned his back on me, and I released a silent sigh of relief. "I thought I heard something."

"You'll do anything not to be introduced to my friends, darling. It's almost painful to watch the lengths you'll go to, to avoid it." She still had her hand on him, and my eyebrows crawled to my hairline when he shook her off.

"Leave," Dimitri snapped before taking a deep breath and rolling his shoulders. The shirt stretched to its limits, and I fully expected him to shift. He didn't. "My father is here, and I need to deal with him. Make sure he doesn't see you on your way out."

"He is the one that agreed to the engagement, if you forgot. I will not be hiding from him." Angela jutted her chin out stubbornly and glared at him. She might not look tough, but she definitely had a spine to stand up to the alpha. Agitated power was rolling off him in waves, blasting my skin.

I could've avoided it, but I was still frozen on the landing. If I understood it correctly, I was witnessing Dimitri Bell hiding his fiancée in a barely lit stairway of his company's building. I filed that in my mind in case I needed to use it against the alpha in the future after I destroyed whatever he had against me. Sharp senses or not, he had no idea I was standing there ready to take away his leverage. Dimitri would be getting the shock of his life before the day was over.

"If you don't leave, you will regret it." Confirming that he was the jerk I suspected him to be, he opened the door and waited for Angela to exit ahead of him. Which she did after huffing an annoyed breath like a petulant child. Pouting, she sashayed through the door with her head held high like she was the Queen of England.

My body tensed to continue down the stairs, avoiding the floor I knew Dimitri was prowling around, when he stepped out and tugged the door behind him. One foot on the stair and the other up, I flinched when he glanced over his shoulder, his stormy eyes locking on mine. There was a promise in his irises that spoke of many things I'd regret before he gently pulled the door closed, and I almost collapsed when my knees buckled. It was impossible for the shifter to see me through the spell. I couldn't see myself when I used it. No matter how many times I told myself the same thing, something deep inside me was screaming for me to run.

So run I did.

Forgetting all about destroying evidence and threats to expose my identity, I bolted out of the building with only one thing in mind: I had to take the book I stole and get it to Dimitri Bell. Something was not right about the whole situation, and I had a sinking feeling my death was the only outcome at the end of this journey. If he had it back, maybe I could pretend I had no idea what he was talking about when it came to it. It was the smartest thing to do.

I had to talk to Char. Stat.

All the way home, I felt eyes stabbing between my shoulder blades, but there was no one around when I glanced over my shoulder.

Great. On top of everything else, now I was getting paranoid, too.

Chapter Six

Char watched me over the rim of her cup without a word. She wasn't drinking the coffee; she was just smelling it while tendrils of steam curled in front of her like dancing cobras. I found her unlocking the front door when I ran back home like a little girl scared of the big bad wolf. Gah! Someone needed to slap me across the head for being stupid. Gnawing on my lower lip, I waited for her to say something. A confirmation that I wasn't crazy, maybe? I couldn't tell for sure.

"And he looked straight at you?" Repeating the words for the umpteenth time, she wrinkled her nose. "Not at your nose or your forehead or something, but locked gazes?" My best friend was still wearing the long black dress she had on for work, not bothering to change when I unloaded my crazy on her.

"Yup." The silence stretched, and I progressed from gnawing on my lower lip to chewing on my nails.

The tap of the kitchen sink in our apartment didn't close properly, so the plop of the water drops in regular intervals echoed in the silence, and the sound was like nails in my brain. It only added to my frustration. Not that we couldn't afford a better place, but we stayed at our old apartment for safety's sake. Both Char and I had placed wards around it for so long that no one in the world had a safer home. Anyone coming with ill intent would be fried before they even reached our front door.

"Rumors are that he is the strongest alpha the pack has ever had, but I doubt he saw through your spell, Allie." She finally lowered the cup and narrowed her dark eyes on me. "My guess is that he knew someone was there but the pinpointing was accidental. He is arrogant enough to pull it off, too."

The vise that had been crushing my lungs since I left Ice Matrix CO. loosened, and I slumped in the chair, making it groan. Deep down, I knew nothing could pierce the invisibility magic, but I needed confirmation to put my mind at ease. Scrubbing a hand over my face, I glanced around the living room and the lived-in furniture in earth tones we picked together what felt like a lifetime ago. Scented candles I powered up with my magic were perched on every flat surface, their flickering flames dancing on a nonexistent breeze. Apart from the calming scents of sage, white tea, and lilacs, they assured every word spoken stayed between the walls. It was the first thing Char did, lighting them, before I spilled everything that happened. Behind the wingback chair I occupied was a narrow hall leading to a bathroom and both our bedrooms, plus a small workshop that Char used to brew her potions when home. Pictures of us on our travels graced the walls, both of us smiling from ear to ear.

A fist clogged my throat.

Accepting the job to steal the book might bring everything we built for ourselves to an end. As much as I appreciated Char's reassurance, there was a nagging feeling in the pit of my stomach warning me that our lives were about to be flipped upside down.

"I'm sure you are right." I continued to do a messy job of butchering my nails with my teeth. "But since my client is not answering his phone after he paid the full fee for it, mind you, I've got half a mind to return the book where it belongs. It's not worth the stress and paranoia. The money is sitting there, and he can have it back when he decides to finally accept my calls."

"If that's what you want, then do it." The grimace on her face didn't match her words. "At this point, I'm not sure it'll make a difference, whether you return it or not. It'll only lead to more trouble if they are expecting you this time around."

"Did you open it?" There was no need to wait for an answer since her expression spoke volumes.

After I told Char what happened while we stared at our lunch instead of eating it, both of us tried to see what the big deal was with the small book. Apart from the powerful magic coming from it, it appeared unassuming and plain. There was absolutely nothing else special about it, until we bent over it and prepared to flip through its pages. No matter what we did, including using potions Char specifically prepared for it, we couldn't open it. She suggested we try offering a few drops of blood as a last resort, but I drew a line at that.

Nothing good came from using blood magic.

"If you really plan on returning it, we should just let it be." My friend scanned the books filling our bookshelves to bursting that lined one entire wall before turning her gaze back on me. "If you are not, I have a couple more ideas we could try."

"I think—" I never got the chance to finish the sentence.

A loud crash came from the hallway in front of our front door. The protective wards around the place lit up like a Christmas tree, prickling my skin with thousands of papercuts. Glass shattered, too, the tinkling sound echoing between my ears like a gong. While I struggled to stand from the chair, Char darted toward her workshop, appearing two seconds later with armfuls of small bottles filled with potions.

"Get the book," she hissed through clenched teeth and planted herself between me and the now-bulging door of our home.

That command got my legs moving, and I rushed to my bedroom, skidding over the wooden floor on my knees until I stopped myself when I reached my bed. Ducking my head under it, I yanked the black plastic suitcase out, thumbing the code to open it. I didn't bother closing it after I snatched the book and my mother's journal. Instead, I jumped to my feet, tucking them into the waistband of my pants under my shirt. The sound of the front door bursting into splinters had me dashing madly toward the living room, the daggers I didn't bother removing from their sheaths already in my hands.

I skidded to a stop.

The scene unfolding before me gave me whiplash. While I had been worried about the shifter pack, along with their alpha, gunning for my head because I dared steal from them, I ended up with a dozen vampires breaking into my home and doing their best to kill my best friend. Out of all supernaturals, vampires were the last in a line of creatures that should be able to bypass the wards.

Char, to her credit, didn't even flinch. Feet planted shoulder-width apart, she chucked potion after potion, nailing each vampire that crossed our threshold right between the eyes. Bright lights like mini suns exploded on their foreheads, setting them on fire, and they flailed around, wind-milling their arms as if that would help them. Taking a couple of steps back for a running start, I jumped over the sofa, spinning around like some psycho ballerina in the air and slashing the daggers through two necks that got in the way. Heads bounced off bodies, the vampires bursting into clouds of ash before they hit the floor. Small piles were already covering the parquet like tiny ant hills a foot or so from our front door.

Landing in a crouch next to Char, I stood and we faced the remaining creatures shoulder to shoulder.

"I have about four more," my best friend said from the corner of her mouth, her voice breaking. It was the only thing showing how scared she was, something no one else would be able to tell by the way she glared fiercely at our attackers.

"On three, cover your eyes."

I saw her sharp nod at my murmur, and I lowered my blades in hopes that the idiots would come closer. They lingered in the hallway, but seeing me step down gave them courage. Whoever was left, made a mad dash for us, and that was all I needed. My mouth opened to utter the spell, but the glimpse of a furry body close to the stairs leading to the floor below gave me pause. Char's scream when one of the vampires raked his claws over her arm snapped me out of it, and with a long breath, I shouted the spell.

"*Leig an solas a-steach.*" "*Let there be light*" was a powerful spell I should not have used, but I had no other choice. The blades of my daggers lit up a second before a blast of bright golden light filled not just the apartment but the entire hallway and stairs outside of it.

The vampires had no time to scream, the glow eviscerating them on impact. Ash floated around us in a macabre curtain of gray flakes when the blast died, leaving bright spots dancing at the corners of my eyes. As the spell dissipated, all the energy in me left in a whoosh, and I dropped on my knees, barely able to keep my head up. My chin kept dropping toward my chest, although Char was there with her arms wrapped around my shoulders to prevent me from face-planting on the dust-covered floor. Blood trickled down her arm before splattering at our feet.

"You did it, Allie." Her usually sultry tone had a hysterical edge to it that didn't sit well with me. Char was never hysterical, no matter what she faced.

With great effort, I lifted my head to assure her it was no big deal, and that we had done it together. A dozen vampires couldn't hold a candle to a badass like her, and she needed to know it, but the words died on my tongue. My gaze found the largest wolf I'd ever seen staring straight at me from the top of the stairs. Midnight fur absorbed all the light around him while he stood unmoving like a statue. Silver blue eyes glittered with an emotion I couldn't name, but before I called out to him, I blinked and he was gone. Shaking my head, I stared a bit longer, debating if I had really saw him or if maybe my imagination was playing tricks on me.

"Allie?" Char shook my shoulders, and, reluctantly, I dragged my eyes to her face. "It's over thanks to you. Can you stand? We need to get the hell out of here."

Since I was unable to talk, I nodded once and swayed as if drunk when I stood. Char balanced me with an arm around my waist, and with one quick glance around the apartment, she shuffled both of us out of there. So much for having the safest home and best wards. But that was the least of my worries. The most important thing I wanted to know was sitting like lead at the pit of my stomach.

Was the alpha in my building to help me, or was he the one who'd brought vampires to my doorstep?

It was time to face the big bad wolf and get the answers I needed.

Chapter Seven

The morning came too fast for my liking, and I muttered curses under my breath while I waddled around the store. I had every intention of staying curled on top of the covers in the shitty motel room we rented for the night, but Char bodily dragged me to work. According to her, dwelling in misery and trying to sleep off my problems would do me no good. I tended to disagree with things like that, but I didn't have it in me to even argue with my friend.

"We need to make a list of things we need to order for the store," Char announced from behind the register where she was furiously typing on the laptop perched on top of the counter. Obviously, it was just me who wasn't allowed to sleep my problems away like nothing was wrong. It was perfectly fine for Char to act like this was just another day in Crystal Palace and we didn't have a bunch of vampires trying to chomp on us the night before.

"*Okay.*" Side-eying her, I lined the candles on the shelf for the third time, nudging them left and right so all of them were visible. "I'm pretty sure we have everything you need to make the healing potion, though. So, how about you go do that instead of placing orders for now?"

Char's upper arm was wrapped in a makeshift bandage we'd ripped from the covers on the bed, which had looked cleaner than the rest of the motel room. The beige color was already stained with blood and forming dark blotches where her skin was raked from the vampire's claws. If my friend was not worried about me, she would've healed herself already, but instead of doing that, she wouldn't leave my side.

"It's nothing." Dismissing me without looking up from the screen, she wiggled on the chair until I couldn't see her injured arm from where I was standing. "It's practically healed on its own. We have a business to run."

One thing I loved about Char was her determination and focus when it came to our success as business owners. The Apocalypse could come and she would be on that damn laptop making sure all deliveries were on time and all the bills were paid. Unlike me. I had no idea which bank we used, little less anything else. A lot of times I wondered why she didn't kick me to the curb and do it herself. She'd have a lot less trouble, that was for sure.

"Char, please." I was not above begging as long as she took care of herself. "I already feel like crap that you got hurt because of my stupidity. Heal your arm for me if you're not going to do it for yourself."

"Fine." With an annoyed huff, she slapped the laptop closed and jumped off the chair. "It's still early, so there shouldn't be a rush until later in the day. I'll be as fast as I can." Halfway to the door leading to the back of the store where her workroom was, she paused, glancing at me over her shoulder. "Call me if you need help, and after lunch, we will stop by the police station to give them our statements." She didn't go until I nodded my agreement.

We stopped at the apartment on our way to the store and found yellow police tape stretched from one end to the other and everything inside our home covered in some type of foam. Someone must've called the cops after we left, and I shuddered just thinking of strangers touching everything we owned. Char had no qualms about it, chatting up a storm about what type of substance the police had used to create the foam for preserving DNA and any prints while she waded through it to reach her room.

Shivers slithered up my spine as I followed behind her, and the moment I filled a duffle with a change of clothing in my room, I couldn't get out of there fast enough. In less than twelve hours, my safe place, my home, had been turned from a safe haven to a space I didn't want anything to do with. I'd be happy if I never saw it again. The bell chiming pulled me from my thoughts, and I realized I was still standing in front of the shelf lined with candles, staring blankly at it.

"Good morning. Welcome to the ..." The smile I plastered as I turned to face the first customer of the day froze on my lips when my eyes locked on an intent silver blue gaze.

My heart did a hard lurch, punching the roof of my mouth before dropping to my toes.

"Indeed a good morning, Miss McCullough." A thick accent made my last name sound a lot more Kalla then it should've.

Dimitri freaking Bell was in my store. Like, inside the store, with his entire body. He actually used his legs and dragged his too-handsome-for-his-own-good self into *my store*. And to make matters worse, he was staring at me with a slight tilt to the corner of his stupid lips like he knew something I didn't.

I was hyperventilating.

"Get out." The words ripped from somewhere deep in my soul and spilled from my mouth.

"I beg your pardon?" One eyebrow arched up as if he couldn't believe my audacity. Oh, he better believe it, because I had more where that came from.

"Begging is forbidden inside a business. Along with soliciting." My body was shaking but from rage, not fear. Clenching my fists, I leaned forward, pushing each word through bared teeth. "Get the hell out of my store." Magic was churning inside me, begging to be unleashed, but I held it back with everything in me. *Don't be stupid, Alaska. That's what he wants, just another confirmation that you are a witch. Don't give him more proof.*

The jerk chuckled. He chuckled!

Whipping my head wildly around, I searched for something heavy to throw at him. Deep down, I knew it was a bad idea, but seeing that infuriating grin on his face made me irrational. Since the closest thing were the candles, I snatched a beautiful healing one made out of indigo organic wax textured with turquoise shards and chucked it at his head. The six-inch-tall candle flipped through the air between us, but after widening his arrogant gaze, he ducked before it could smack him in the forehead. It hit a glass display behind him instead, sending crystals and incense holders flying everywhere as they crashed on the floor. Another candle was already in my hand, this one for prosperity and made with forest green wax that was textured with larger pieces of citrine.

Dimitri stepped aside from its trajectory when I threw it hard enough to make a professional baseball pitcher envious, and the candle shattered a shelf full of small statues. Porcelain, glass, wood, and crystals littered the floor and the very strong scent of peppermint saturated the air. A pang stabbed my chest when I realized my attempts for pitcher of the year had shattered a few bottles of pure essential oils. It took months, sometimes years to get one small bottle filled.

A red haze colored my vision, while the ass who dared to come inside my store, after threatening to expose me and sending vampires to kill me, tugged on the sleeves of his shirt to straighten invisible wrinkles on his immaculate suit.

"We need to talk." Whatever else he was going to say was drowned by another glass display exploding when one more candle missed his head. "I see this is the wrong time for a conversation." Dimitri glared at me disapprovingly like everything was my fault.

"Allie." Char came running from the back of the store and skidded to a stop when she saw me facing off with the alpha, my right arm cocked back with yet another candle clutched tightly in my hand. A blood red one for reigniting the passion between lovers. Shards of rose quartz as large as my thumb jutted out of it, and they were sharp enough to poke his eye out if I hit my target. "Allie, no," my friend shouted, her arm outstretched like she could magically pull away my weapon made out of organic wax. Fortunately for me, I was the witch, not Char.

Dimitri had his head turned toward my friend, and I took advantage of it. The candle sailed through the air, and every inch it passed forming a smile on my face. At the last second, the alpha jerked his head around, and it missed him by a breath. One jutting shard sliced a line across his high cheekbone, and blood beaded on the cut immediately. Char sucked in a sharp breath that was too loud in the deathly silent store, while Dimitri's eyes flashed with a dangerous light.

I stopped breathing.

All the anger drained out of me in an instant and replaced itself with dread. The shifter was over six feet tall and wide enough to block the door of the store with his shoulders. I had no delusions that he could crush me with his bare hands if he wanted. I knew he could.

One glass shelf that was knocked aside chose that moment to lose its battle against gravity, and I jumped a foot off of the ground when it crashed to the floor. So did Char, for that matter, but at least she landed in a crouch, ready to tackle the alpha if he attacked. Unlike me. I was focused on not peeing my panties at that point. Stunned, I watched owlishly when Dimitri raised his hand and wiped the blood trickling down his cheekbone with his thumb, all the while not taking his intense gaze from me. My body was gently rocking back and forth from the strength of my heartbeat, which was bruising my ribs.

"Meet me in an hour at the corner of the Pier, Miss McCullough." His baritone vibrated in my chest, along with my frantic heartbeat. "Hopefully you will come to your senses by then. As I said, we need to talk."

His suit jacket, as well as the white shirt he wore, were stretched over his torso to their limit. The alpha was fighting not to shift in the middle of my store, and that was the only reason I nodded frantically like an idiot. I could fight with the man on any day of the week. His wolf was a whole different matter. Reasoning with a person was easier than trying to reason with an animal. Even in my moment of insanity, I knew that all too well. With one last long look to make sure I understood the threat clearly written in his eyes, Dimitri turned around and stormed out of the store.

The moment the front door closed with the bell chiming happily above it, I collapsed on the floor. Char darted my way, dropping on her knees next to me when the door opened again and the alpha returned. I wanted to die because he saw me on my knees, and I was about to struggle back to my feet when his frown stopped me. Something passed through his gaze that was too fast to decipher because he looked away. Bending down, he snatched something and left for good that time.

"Why did he come back?" Char tightened her arms around my shoulders, talking more to herself than me.

My eyes roved over the floor until I found what was missing. Leaning my forehead on her shoulder, I hugged her back, the familiar scent of the fruity lotion she always used calming me.

"He took the candle," I mumbled in her hair. The bastard took the red candle that I used to draw his blood.

I was so screwed.

Chapter Eight

"Take this." My friend shoved a small round bottle full of silvery liquid at me. "He so much as comes a foot from you, smash it over his head."

"What is it?" Turning it between my fingers, I watched the liquid roll inside it. "It's not just going to piss him off, right? It'll knock his ass down?"

"Better." Smiling like a villain, she wiggled her perfectly shaped eyebrows. "It'll melt the skin off his bones."

Flinching back, I jabbed it at her chest. "Hell no. Take it back. Are you trying to get us killed?"

"Don't be daft. We are dead either way after you drew his blood in the middle of the store. This way, at least we can get a head start on running."

"It came to that, didn't it?" Groaning, I scrubbed a hand over my face. "Maybe we should just grab whatever we can and disappear. After a while, he might give up and stop coming after us."

I had half an hour left until I had to meet with the alpha for his, as he called it, talk. We put valid effort into cleaning up the mess, but after ten minutes, we closed the store for the day. Both of us were too wired to be able to get it in order or deal with people after the fiasco early in the morning.

"We are not letting him chase us away, Allie." Char tugged my blouse down like a mother straightening the clothes of her six-year-old for their first day at school. "First, we will see what he has to say for himself, then we make a plan of action. We will defend our turf."

"We are a gang now?" Slapping her hands away when she tried to straighten the collar of my blouse, I glared at her. "We are defending turfs?"

"This is our home town. We will defend it." Jutting her chin out stubbornly, she folded her arms across her chest.

"I'm a thief, Char, not a ninja." Scratching my head, I grimaced when I pulled a tiny shard of glass from my hair.

"Could've fooled me." Snickering, she ran her fingers through my hair, searching for more stray glass that could've wedged in it. "You should've seen yourself with the candles. I was scared."

"So embarrassing." My groan was punctuated by peals of laughter bursting out of her. "I have no idea what possessed me."

"You were defending your turf. We might get matching jackets while we are at it, too." That time, I joined her when she snorted. "And you are not just a thief, my friend. You are a witch—a very powerful one, may I remind you? If that jerk wants a war, he will get it."

"And both of us will die because of it. Me, for being a witch, and you, for hiding one." It was the truth and she knew it.

"I don't know what you are talking about. Alaska

McCullough is a candlemaker, and I have the candles to prove it, too."

"I better go before he decides to come back here." My feet didn't want to move, but if I didn't meet the alpha at the place of his choosing, I had no doubts he would be knocking on the door. Doing what he wanted would ensure he stayed away from Char.

"One second." Darting around the counter, Char tugged her tote from under it and hitched it over her shoulder. "Okay, let's go."

"Where do you think you are going?" I regretted planting my fists on my hips when the cut on my knuckles scraped the fabric. That would teach me to throw candles around glass again. I should've just poured hot wax over Dimitri's head, and if I knew he'd be coming to the store, I would've had it ready.

Like I had not spoken, Char was already at the door, holding it open for me to exit. With a sigh, I followed her, knowing too well the wolf wouldn't be happy if I showed up late for our rendezvous. People were out and about, their cheerful chatter and laughter building up the dread in my stomach hard enough I felt I could barely walk. But walk I did, dragging my feet one in front of the other until only a long stretch of sand stood between me and the man I could recognize anywhere at that point. With a comforting squeeze to my shoulder, Char veered off to the right in search of a good place she could hunker down and chuck her potions at Dimitri if he got handsy. Or at least that was what she told me in any case.

The man in question stood on the beach just to the side of the Ferris Wheel, hands folded behind him and his back toward me. If that wasn't a sign he wasn't scared of me, I didn't know what was. Never turn your back on a worthy opponent was a motto Char and I lived by. The alpha made sure I was aware I was a joke compared to him. Jaw clenched and hands balled at my sides, I joined him, my flats kicking up tiny clouds of sand as I stomped across the beach.

"Here I am, your Majesty. Talk." My hiss did not impress him one bit, and I could tell.

"How did I miss your presence in my city so far, malen'kaya ved'ma?" Dimitri, his accent thick at the last words, murmured under his breath, but he didn't look at me. The impressive silver gaze roved over the ocean where waves were lapping across the vast expanse of water.

"If you are going to insult me, at least do it in English so I can repay the favor, wolf." That earned me one of the chuckles I heard in the store. My palm itched to slap the smile off his face.

"We have a problem, Miss McCullough." The alpha ignored me, as I expected he would. His wide shoulders turned slightly, just enough so he could peer at me from his greater height. I was five foot six, not very short, but compared to him I looked like a child. The top of my head barely reached his shoulder.

I hated it.

"You mean you have a problem and decided to drag others along for the ride." My hand drifted toward my thigh where one of my daggers waited. I placed a glamour so no one would know I was armed, yet my heart stuttered in my chest when Dimitri's eyes dropped to it as if he could see the blade as plain as day.

"You should not have touched the book."

It took me aback the way he said it. I fully expected the shifter to threaten, rage, or snarl at me. Huffing, puffing, and other such things I associated with the wolf. But he didn't do any of those things. If anything, he sounded tired and weary.

"I don't know what you are talking about, Mr. Bell." Taking a lesson from his book, I figured maybe formalities would help send him on his way. "All I know is I was attacked by vampires in my own home and you were there. Then you have the decency to show up at my store."

"You recognize my wolf." It wasn't a question, but I found myself answering anyway.

"It's kinda hard to miss. It's huge."

Dimitri narrowed his piercing gaze on me as if he was trying to read my mind. Arching my eyebrow, I dared him to contradict me, but we both knew no shifter was the size of his beast. Well, none that I'd ever seen anyway. The night when we were attacked, I might've doubted what I saw, but it cleared out when I woke up. Dimitri Bell was in my building when the bloodsuckers attacked. At least he didn't deny it.

"Who hired you to steal the book?" The shifter could give me whiplash the way he was jumping from one topic to another.

"What book?" Blinking innocently at him, I wanted to laugh when a low growl rumbled from his chest.

"Let me be clear, Miss McCullough." His whole body turned my way, and I had to suffer the full weight of his gaze. Like a physical sensation, it pressed on my chest and shoulders like an anvil, and I had to struggle to breathe normally. "I know what you are."

All the blood drained from my face, numbing my lips, but he kept talking.

"In good faith, I will tell you that I, too, have witch blood in my veins. My grandmother was a witch, just like you." White noise thudded in my ears, making his deep voice come from far away, but I heard that loud and clear. "It is the reason I was raised in my mother's homeland. The sigils you saw when you stole the book were placed there by me. After you used your power in that room, I can find your magic anywhere. Now you know my secret, the same way I know yours. So, let me ask again. Where is the book?"

I understood what he was doing, but my mind was stuck on one thing. "You are a witch?" I asked him dumbly, blinking a million miles an hour like that would change the absurdity of the situation.

"I am a wolf." Ducking his head to stare me in the eye, he glared.

As if it had a mind of its own, my finger stabbed the air at his nose. "But you have witch magic, too."

"I do." A muscle danced the Macarena at the edge of his square jaw.

At that, I did the dumbest thing I could think of.

I laughed.

Chapter Nine

"I fail to see what is funny in this situation." Dimitri seemed insulted but I couldn't stop laughing to save my life. What was worse: I went as far as bending over and gasping for air. "Stop that this instant," the shifter barked at me in annoyance.

He could take his alpha commands and stick them up his perfectly rounded and firm behind for all I cared, but he made the mistake of touching me. Strong fingers wrapped around my shoulder, and the pad of his thumb ended up pressed on the skin of my collarbone. A current passed between us, rattling my very essence. We jumped away from each other like we'd been burned, warily eyeing one another from a few feet away.

I was no longer laughing.

Tiny zaps were still coursing under my skin and raising goosebumps in their wake, although the bastard was far enough away. My mind was spinning to find the meaning of it, but I decided it didn't matter. I had bigger things to worry about when it came to Dimitri Bell.

"What's funny about all this is the fact you think I'm an idiot." While I kept my distance, I didn't need to speak out loud. His shifter hearing would hear me even if I whispered. "That you honestly believed if you told me some fairytale story about your grandmother being a witch, I'd do what exactly? Admit all my sins and share all my secrets?" The tone of my voice should've insulted him more than any colorful words I could've used.

"I spoke the truth." With a shake of his head, he pinched the bridge of his straight nose between a thumb and a forefinger. I wanted to do a wiggle dance for the fact that I gave him a headache. "We are wasting time here. I will have the book back, Miss McCullough, I assure you of that. What I want to know, however, is who hired you to take it from me."

"Assuming that I am the one who stole it." I didn't miss my chance to point that out in case he thought I was admitting to any of his accusations. "For your information, I'm a candlemaker, which you can feel free to ask my business partner. I'm sure she'll be happy to set your mind at ease."

"Ah, yes. Charmaine Mariatti. A sorceress well known for hard to find potions and talismans on the black market. I'm sure she will be more than happy to tell me the truth," Dimitri drawled, sarcasm thick in the tone of his voice. I prayed to everything that he didn't notice the blow he'd dealt me with that information. Char was selling illegal potions on the black market? Say what now?

I had no ground to stand on, so I couldn't judge my friend no matter what she did, but I'd be lying if I said it didn't hurt. We agreed to never ask questions about our powers and such, but the fact that she knew I was a thief but hid things from me smarted like hell. Not that I'd show Dimitri that by any means.

My shoulder twitched in what I hoped was a devil-may-care shrug. "I don't see why she wouldn't." Spreading my arms wide and my palms up, I took a step away from him. "As I said, I make candles. If you need one for ... I don't know, to get your passion going between you and your fiancée, just come by the shop. I got you covered. Until then, I'm out." Spinning on my heel, I had barely taken a couple of steps when he spoke.

"How do you know about my engagement?"

My eyes closed.

Char always told me that my big mouth would eventually get me in so much trouble no number of spells or magic would be able to get me out of it. I proved her right the first chance I got. Yay, me. The dumbass who blurted everything that came to mind, including things I shouldn't know.

I faced him but kept walking backward. "Huh? I was just saying. When you do get engaged or whatever. Call me psychic I guess." My nervous laugh turned into a squeal when he snatched me by the wrist. I'd heard of shifters moving fast, but Dimitri pulled some vampire speed to materialize next to me in less then a second. "Let go of me."

A few people who dared to walk near where we were standing gave us fleeting glances, but no one came to my rescue. I couldn't blame them because Dimitri, although dressed in a suit, was more intimidating than a vampire baring his fangs at everyone. I'd stay away if I was them, too.

The alpha didn't release my wrist. In fact, his fingers tightened almost painfully.

"I'm not a shifter, but if you don't remove your hand from me, I'll bite it off," I told him calmly and stopped struggling to yank my arm out of his grip.

"Or you could use your magic to free yourself, krasivaya." When his baritone vibrated inside my chest, I realized how close we stood to each other. His scent, something untamed and wild, filled my nose, and subconsciously, my body leaned toward him.

"That would be very stupid if I was, as you like to accuse me of being a witch."

It was the best course of action to ignore the breathless tone of my voice. My eyes lifted from his chest toward his face, and my breath left in a whoosh when I locked them on his gaze. His silver blue irises were stormy and dark as his lips parted slightly. I stopped breathing when his head lowered, but much to my frustration, he stopped before he kissed me. I felt his warm breath grazing my skin.

"Or maybe it would be smart," he murmured, and a bright glow illuminated the space between us.

With great effort, I dragged my eyes away from his lips to look down. When I did, my whole body jerked back, but he had an iron grip on my wrist holding me in place. Magic glowed in the palm of his free hand trapped between us. Witch magic. And the idiot was using it out in the open in broad daylight.

"Put it away." My hiss made him grumble something in what I guessed was Russian, but he did listen. "What the hell is the matter with you? Do you want to die?"

"Now you know I spoke the truth. Da?" Well, I knew what that last part meant at least. Look at me, all worldly and what not.

"Da," I answered him instead of saying yes, and made sure I layered mocking into my tone. I felt like an idiot for thinking he was going to kiss me when all he was doing was hiding the fact he was performing witch magic in front of everyone. That frustrated me more than anything.

"Now, will you tell me where the book is?" Dimitri took

pity on my pathetic self and stepped back. With the heat of his body away from me, I could finally breathe, so I rolled my shoulders and pretended his nearness was annoying. I'd die before he knew I actually liked it.

Pathetic.

"Why is this book so important?" Despite all my misgivings, I had to ask. "It's a magical object. You, of all people, have enough money to buy ten of those at any time." The sky started darkening, which was weird for the middle of the day, and I glanced up at the gray clouds rolling over our heads. I think that was the only reason he answered, his face tilted up as he frowned at the sky.

"It belonged to my grandmother. Inside it is our family tree with every name written where the magic was passed from generation to generation." His handsome face turned my way, and the blood curdled in my veins. "Including mine. Whoever hired you to steal it could ruin not just everything my father has built. They could ruin me, too, along with my pack."

"Oh, shit." Hands shaking, I struggled to swallow the lump that squeezed my windpipe.

"Where is the book, Alaska?" Hearing my name rolling off his tongue in his thick accent had my knees buckling. The idiotic butterflies sprang into action in my belly, and I had to force myself to stay standing instead of melting into a puddle on the sand.

My mouth opened to tell him I had the book safe, but I never got the chance to voice the words.

The world around us exploded.

Chapter Ten

"Elementals," Dimitri snarled, his head swiveling around searching for the mages.

People screamed, and panic made them run wildly around us like chickens with their heads cut off. The bright blue sky from a moment ago was replaced by thick dark clouds that churned ominously right above our heads. Lightning spiderwebbed over them, and a clap of thunder shook the ground under my feet. To make matters worse, the ocean pulled back, rising in a monstrous wave behind us. Panic had me frozen in place, and no amount of internal screaming could get my feet moving.

"Run." He grabbed my arm and shoved me toward the walkway that circled around the beach. I stumbled for a couple of steps but didn't listen. "Run, woman. Go!"

Two figures appeared a few yards in front of us, dressed in black cloaks with elaborate golden thread swirling on the fabric. The one on the left had his arms raised toward the sky, and the one on the right had them leveled up front as if reaching for the ocean. At least we knew which mage controlled what element. Without thinking, my fingers wrapped around the hilts of my daggers, and I pulled them out as I stepped shoulder to shoulder with Dimitri. Well, shoulder to chest, really, but who cared?

"What are you doing?" The alpha looked at me like I'd sprouted two heads.

"What does it look like I'm doing, wolf?" Even shitless scared, I had my bravado going for me. The daggers swirled in my hands. "Protecting another witch." My lips stretched into a wicked smile.

"This does not make us allies." He had the gall to throw that at me like I was dying to be buddies with him.

"Don't flatter yourself." The tip of my dagger pointed at the mages. "They attacked me first. This has nothing to do with you."

In reality, it had everything to do with the alpha. Whoever it was that paid me to steal the book knew that it was still in my possession. After the chitchat with the wolf, I was sure it was my client sending vampires and then mages to attack. With Dimitri by my side, my chances of survival were higher than trying to take them on my own. If nothing else, at least Char was safe at that moment. Fate had to screw that up for me, too, because the mentioned sorceress came out of nowhere and bolted in my direction, her large tote flapping on her butt.

"No. Char, go back." My shout had her running faster toward me instead of turning around.

"Women." The jerk next to me shook his head.

"If you continue that sentence, you'll be the first person I stab today." Brandishing a dagger in his direction, I glared at him. Another bolt of lightning streaked above our heads, and a louder clap of thunder rattled my organs.

"Mages." Char panted as she reached us, a hand

pressed to her chest. And like I was blind, she also pointed at the two cloaked figures that were much closer than before.

"Thank you, Captain Obvious. Now go hide." I nudged her with my elbow, careful not to slash her with the dagger.

"Like hell I'll hide." Char slapped my elbow away with a frown. "I didn't want him to know I was here." Her chin jutted toward Dimitri. "I don't give a rat's ass if those two see me." Her hand was already inside the tote almost to her shoulder while she rummaged through it.

From the corner of my eye, I noticed Dimitri giving my friend an assessing once-over. Whatever he saw must've been good because he nodded at Char once and turned to face the elementals. Far be it for me to complain about help. Warily, I glanced at the ten-story-high wave behind us, trembling ominously. My biggest fear was drowning, as irrational as it was. Seeing that much water just waiting to cover me had my heart working overtime and my lungs struggling to fill with air. I'd take my chances fighting anyone as long as the ocean stayed where it belonged. As always, the thoughts had come too soon.

The mage on the right slashed his palms down, and the sand under my feet shifted. I heard the ocean like the sound of a distant train whooshing behind me, but I had no time to escape. On my right, there was nothing but flat sand and a line of low buildings while the pier with the humongous Ferris Wheel was blocking us from the left. A calm settled over me with the fact that my worst nightmare was about to come true. My hold on the daggers tightened as if that would protect me from what was coming.

Tons of gallons of water crushed over me.

My hip and shoulder took the brunt of the hit when the ocean pressed me on the sand. My head bounced off the packed ground before I was tossed to the side like a rag doll. Everything in me wanted to scream, but I forced my lips shut while my lungs protested because I was holding my breath. Dark, murky water swirled around me, sending tendrils of my red hair floating around my face like streaks of blood. The weight of the daggers I still clutched like an anchor in my hands was the only thing keeping me sane. Why didn't I run? What possessed me to stay by that arrogant jerk's side when I didn't want anything to do with him? I killed Char, too, with my dumb decisions.

Oh dear abyss, Char!

The ocean didn't stand a chance. Guilt was going to drown me faster.

My heart skipped a beat when a large dark shape passed near me, and I slashed with my dagger, but it was so slow it disappeared before my arm was halfway up. I hid my powers and magic the best I could, and it never dawned on me to learn a spell about breathing under water.

Or moving freely while inside an ocean. I only knew what was useful for my trade. I was going to die because of ignorance. *And arrogance*, a voice suspiciously sounding like Char's chirped in my head.

The breath that I was selfishly holding burst out of me when something hit me in the stomach and took me away with it to the side. Unable to stop myself, I sucked in a mouthful of salty water and kicked my legs weakly when my throat burned. Instead of expelling it, I kept drinking more and more in my panic, and dark spots danced at the corners of my eyes. Just when I thought it was the end, whatever had me broke the surface of the water, and cold air slapped me across the face.

I choked.

Water gushed out of my mouth in large streams, and I

coughed so hard my chest and stomach hurt like a bull had gone to town on my torso. It felt like forever until I realized two things. My back was pressed to a wooden beam where I had one arm wrapped around it and clung to it like a monkey. Second, was my other hand was tangled in thick, dark fur, and something large was holding me up. When the tears stopped streaming down my face and I stopped trying to cough up my lungs, I looked down through the strands of hair plastered over my face.

My eyes locked on a furious silver blue gaze.

"Dimitri?" Rasping, I blinked fast to make sure I wasn't imagining things. The wolf growled, his upper lip curling over his razor sharp teeth. "Char?" My friend's name choked me all over again. I followed the direction of the wolf's gaze to the side where a figure was draped over the wooden beams. It was clutching a tote, which was wrapped around one arm.

I sagged where I was pressed to the unforgiving, hard surface.

The ocean was going nuts behind the alpha. Waves were raising and slamming down wildly, sending harsh sprays of mist to pelt our skin. Logically, I knew he couldn't communicate with me while in his animal form, but the silence after I asked about my best friend was killing me, although I knew he pulled her out first. I was beyond grateful for that. I breathed easier until the wolf moved away from me and started crawling up the wooden beams crisscrossing behind me. When he came level with me, his jaw closed around my soaking wet shirt, and he tugged me up.

Since I could do nothing else, I flipped around and crawled alongside him. Tears ran unchecked down my face, and I didn't bother wiping them. Char was alive, but that didn't make me feel better at all. The higher I climbed, the more familiar everything became. I realized Dimitri dragged me to the pier after his heroic rescue, and that was what we were climbing. The momentary grief was replaced by anger, and I redoubled my efforts. Reaching the top, I flopped over the edge on my back before rolling to my knees. In my pathetic attempt of drowning, I lost one of my daggers. It must've slipped from my hand, but that was something I could definitely fix. While I fought my panic under water, it was hard to focus on magic, which was no longer the case. I got on my feet at the same time the wolf joined me, and we faced the mages together.

"*Thig air ais.*" *"Come back."* With one arm outstretched toward the churning ocean, I called on my dagger. It lifted from the slapping water and flew into my palm, its weight settling there. I no longer cared who saw my magic or who found out I was a witch. Refusing to turn toward the ocean that had tried to take my life and my friend from me, I zeroed in on the two mages.

"Let's kill them." Without waiting on the wolf, I sprinted down the length of the pier.

Chapter Eleven

A gust of wind jerked me off the ground and tossed me aside like a dish rag. I flew butt over head until I hit the earth hard, rolling a few feet before smacking into the railing. The Ferris Wheel groaned behind us when metal smacked over metal, and I saw Dimitri's wolf rake lines in the pavement with his claws in a futile attempt to stay on the ground. Water pelted us from all sides of the pier, my skin prickling from the sound of the ocean preparing to swallow us whole again. Char was still dangling on the side, and I had to do something before the water mage decided to use her as his toy.

Dimitri clawed his way closer to me, the hulking frame of the wolf blotting out the sky and the ominous clouds. His dark fur was soaking wet and plastered to his body, but the back of his neck was raised as he bristled from being tossed around, I had no doubt. My heart stuttered when the silver blue gaze started to glow on the wolf's face, and a shimmer of blood red magic formed an aura around him. Was he trying to help or get us both killed with his blatant display of magic? I had no right to talk, obviously, but at least I kept the light show to a minimum. Not once had I allowed the color of my powers to manifest the way he was at that moment.

"Slow down on the lights, Rudolph," I hissed at him as I rolled on my stomach. "We can't see past the first line of buildings. There could be people from MPO lurking around."

The wolf didn't look very happy about my reference to Santa's reindeer judging by his curled upper lip as he snarled at me. Apart from that, he couldn't contradict me about the MPO agents. They were like shadows popping out when you least expected them. My life was already taking a nosedive without having those idiots breathing down my neck.

I had to tuck one of my daggers at the small of my back so I could get a firm grip on the railing. With Dimitri pressing on my left and a good hold on my right, we pushed forward toward the end where the Pier met the edge of the beach. A pang stabbed me in my chest when a snicker floated above the churning water of the ocean in my line of sight. It belonged to a child, and I hoped it was forgotten on the beach when the parents grabbed their little one and escaped. I had to believe that, or I would've curled up where I stood.

"We need to get there." Shouting to be heard over the constant hum of the ocean and the thunder clapping above our heads, I pointed the tip of the dagger at the part where the asphalt met the sand. My eyes were stinging like hell every time I blinked from all the sand sticking to my eyeballs.

The small clearing I was indicating was our only chance. Between the ocean water and the wind, the patch of land was unaffected thanks to the two buildings protecting it on either side. We could cast spells without interruption, and that's what we needed if we were going to stop the crazy mages. They didn't look like they had any intention of slowing down until we were dead.

Dimitri didn't wait to ask for permission, which in any other case would've made me angry enough to breathe smoke through my nostrils. The wolf tucked his shoulder behind my knee and, as I lost my balance, he ducked around me so I fell over his back. He plowed toward the patch of land between the buildings, and I held on with a one-handed death grip on his fur. My head was too close to the ground for comfort, and my hair swept the dirt like a broom each time his hind legs pushed off the ground.

Stumbling off the growling alpha when we reached our spot, I glared to make sure he knew I was upset about him toppling me over him like a sack of potatoes. No self-respecting witch liked to be manhandled like that, be it by the wolf or the man himself.

With a deep breath, I reached my free hand toward the two cloaked figures that had turned to keep us in sight. A soft glow started pulsing around them when they realized their mistake for leaving this part undisturbed, and I could feel their magic intensifying. I had a few seconds to rig their powers before a fresh hell opened for us. Dimitri could rip them to ribbons if they were closer, but we both knew there was no way to reach them before they killed us. Multiple lightning bolts were spiderwebbing across the clouds, gaining in power.

"Socair an èadhar, socair an uisge." "Calm the air, calm the water." Palm raised with my fingers splayed as far as they would go, I pushed as much strength as I could into my magic.

The mages startled when the winds died down and the ocean dropped, retreating off the beach. It didn't take them long to recover, and my feet slid a few inches back when they pushed against me. The water mage gave up on lifting the ocean and focused on the moisture in the air and the water drenching my clothing. The fabric tightened like a python around me so suddenly my arm dropped and I lost control of the spell.

One of the lightning bolts flickering above us shot from the clouds straight for the place I stood. The wolf pounced and tackled me to the side of one of the buildings. My head smacked the wall with a sickening thud, but I still didn't miss the hit of thunder when it slammed into the concrete on the exact spot I'd occupied a split second ago. A bright light blinded me, replacing the dancing spots on the edges of my vision.

Dimitri growled next to me, displaying his rage, but unfortunately for both of us, the alpha had to rely on me to deal with the murderous mages. If he'd stayed in his human form, he could've fought them with his magic, but I had no time to ask him why he shifted. He still glowed with that red shimmer around him, however—another thing that made no sense. It didn't do anything to help us.

Blinking fast, I scrambled to my feet and swayed. Dizziness almost swept the feet from under me, but it passed just as fast. Acid burned the back of my throat, another indicator that I probably had a concussion, and just one more hassle I had to deal with later. I had to stay alive if I wanted to suffer the pain. There was a warm trickle under my hair just behind my left ear that I ignored, as well. Tucking my hand behind me, I pulled the second dagger from my waistband and pointed both blades at the mages.

"*Socair an èadhar, socair an uisge.*" "*Calm the air, calm the water."* My shout was so loud, I felt my magic burst not just from the blades but through my lips, too.

The air vibrated as it passed through my mouth with the power, and it rippled in waves in front of my eyes. In a blast, it sailed toward the mages, and when it reached them, both their bodies were thrown back a few feet. They landed on their backs at the same time the wolf yelped from somewhere behind me. It should've been something that alerted me to stop, but I was beyond rational thought. It was moments like these that made me regret allowing my temper to rule me, but it never stopped me from reacting.

"Tha an cumhachd agam a-nis." "I now have your power." The words sounded like they were not my own. My low tone soaked in magic echoed between me and my attackers, and the power I sent toward them started moving back.

For those who could see magic, it'd be like watching a scene on rewind, only with blue and yellow tendrils snaking from the mages and heading my way. Without thinking, I drained the magic from the mages, making it my own. As the last speck of the blue and yellow power was absorbed by my skin, the two magic users slumped back where they were screaming and struggling to stand up. They were human for all intents and purposes. I took their magic, and they would never get it back. Another reason why witches were exterminated like vermin.

And I showed what I was capable of in front of Dimitri.

The thought slammed inside my head like a brick.

Very slowly, I turned around to face the alpha. The wolf was crouched low, the point of his snarling jaw nearly touching the ground. Ears pinned to the back of his skull and hackles raised, his eyes glowed menacingly at me. With my heart in my throat and no sudden movement, I tucked the daggers into their sheaths strapped to my thighs and lifted both hands up in a placating gesture, my fingers curled into fists. The worst thing a witch could do was open her hands toward someone the way humans did in a sign of surrender. It was the strongest way to cast magic with our open palms, and I didn't want Dimitri to clamp his jaw around my neck if he thought I was attacking him.

"I can explain." Keeping my tone calm, I stood still, barely breathing. "I had to stop them before they killed us. I've never done this before."

Dimitri growled deep in his chest, his gaze boring into mine as if he could see my soul.

"I swear it on my life, I've never taken anyone's power before." Which was the honest truth, but I had no idea how to convince him. He had no reason to trust me. I'd stolen from him, after all. Maybe not his power, but a family journal I had no right to touch.

Tears prickled the back of my eyes, but I refused to let them fall. Instead, I blinked fast in an attempt to push them back. My heart was kicking wildly in my chest, and there was a tremor passing through me that I had no way of controlling. It could've been one or all those things that made the alpha give me a chance to explain instead of attacking. A bright flash of light made me flinch and close my eyes. When I opened them, my jaw unhinged and hit the charred pavement at my feet.

Dimitri stood in front of me in all his naked glory.

Chapter Twelve

After staring at me like I'd grown three more heads for over ten minutes while I struggled to keep my eyes on his face and not let them drop to his groin—which they were persistent on doing—we collected Char and returned to the shop. It turned out only the immediate area around the pier had been affected by the storms the air and water mage created, while everything else was left untouched. We heard a few murmurs that it appeared like night had fallen in just that small part of the beach, and no one could see anything that happened inside it.

I nearly cried from happiness.

No one apart from Dimitri and now two humans who used to be mages knew my secret. Not even Char saw me do the unthinkable, thank the stars. What was I thinking? I wasn't thinking, and that was the biggest problem I had. And if Dimitri's face was anything to go by, I'd be paying the price.

"Here." Lips folded inward, I had to bite hard so I could stop myself from smiling.

Dimitri took the blue silky sarong with fringe I handed him, and with a glare that dared me to laugh, wrapped it around his narrow waist. I picked the blue one, like that would make it look more masculine. He walked the entire stretch from the pier to my store in his birthday suit without blinking an eye, while everyone gawked at him, most of them drooling. The alpha appeared very comfortable showing off the merchandise, but I blushed for him hard enough I could've sworn the tips of my ears were on fire.

The silky wrap should've looked dumb on the muscular man, but he pulled it off better than a freaking runway model. His tanned skin glowed under the lights of the store like he'd oiled it, and the dips and bumps of his muscles cast shadows over the expanse of exposed skin. A tingle started low in my belly as I watched him, something that I strangled into submission momentarily. I had bigger problems than a naked, mouthwatering shifter dressed in a silky sarong standing in the middle of my store with his hands propped on his hips. I caught Char tilting her head and almost toppling off the chair behind the register when she tried to check out his behind. My glare made her jerk upright with a bashful expression on her face. I forced her to sit there since she was too rattled by the whole drowning attempt and her skin had a pale tint instead of its usual olive complexion.

"I can give you a t-shirt too if you'd like, but I doubt any of them will fit you," I told the alpha, staring at the tip of his nose because I had no guts to meet his gaze. Between my fingers, I had one of the said shirts pinched to hold it up for him. It had "I went to bitch school" written on it in bright red.

Dimitri glared at me.

My shrug was twitchy and nervous, although I did try to

appear nonchalant. Offering the t-shirt was more for my sake than his if we got technical, but I failed to convince him to cover himself. With all that skin showing, he was too distracting to have a serious conversation with. If I didn't know for a fact that he couldn't talk to me in his wolf form, I would've asked him to shift.

"Here is what we are going to do." The alpha spoke between his teeth. I should've been grateful he was keeping tight control of his anger, but I bristled, nonetheless.

"And what may that be?" With a saccharine smile plastered on my face, I blinked at him innocently.

"You will bring the book to me, along with the name of who hired you to steal it, by midnight tomorrow." His silver blue gaze was hard and unyielding on me. "Don't make the mistake of thinking you can escape me, Miss McCullough." He glanced pointedly at Char, who was staring at the register while it was obvious she was straining her ears to hear every word we exchanged.

And we were back to formalities now that we were no longer in danger of dying. I shouldn't have missed him addressing me by name, yet it stabbed me like a poker at the center of my chest. I knew I was being dumb, but I couldn't help it. Dimitri Bell was every woman's dream, and I was a hot-blooded woman, after all.

It rubbed me all sorts of wrong.

He threatened you, idiot. And he is engaged. No matter how sternly I repeated it in my head, it didn't help. I found my eyes lingering on him like a moth to a flame. So stupid.

"I have no intention of running from anyone, Mr. Bell," I lied slyly. I had every intention of hightailing it the second he turned his back on the store. "As I told you, I never ask the names of my clients. That is something I'm not going to be able to help you with. As for the book, if you give me five minutes, you can have it."

From the corner of my eye, I watched Char reach her hand inside the tote under the counter at her knees, something the alpha didn't miss either. My friend might've been petrified by the attack and rattled from the brush with death, but I had no doubt she would attack Dimitri if he so much as twitched in my direction. How her too-large bag survived the attack by the water mage was a mystery to me.

Dimitri opened his mouth but thought better of it. A line formed between his brows, and he turned his calculating stare from me to Char for a few moments before centering the full weight of it on my face. Apprehension spiked my heartbeat, and cold sweat beaded around my hairline and on my upper lip. I offered to give him back the book. Why wouldn't he just take it and leave?

"By tomorrow midnight, Miss McCullough. The book and the name. If you are not there with both, I'll make sure every agent of MPO is on your tail. It'll be a witch hunt." The grin tilting his lips sent a chill through me and turned my blood to ice. "Ladies." He dipped his head in a short nod and turned to leave.

A million protests sprang to my tongue, but none of them passed my lips. Numb, I watched him saunter out of the store like he owned the place, his shoulders swinging with each step he took. For the first time, I noticed the tattoo stretching across his back, inked with full color. A large black wolf was baying at the full moon, and tendrils of red magic swirled around it. Next to the howling animal was a woman with her right hand tangled in the wolf's fur and her left hand raised toward the moon. The heart shriveled in my chest when I saw strands of red hair dancing around her face and dark green eyes intently locked on the wolf.

Goosebumps pebbled my body, and I jumped a foot off the floor when the bell chimed shrilly before the door closed with a resounding thump.

"Did you—" Char started, but I cut her off harshly.

"Don't." My snap was angry, but all my apprehension and fear was misplaced. It wasn't her fault that my life was about to end. And what in the world was that tattoo? As far as I was aware, Dimitri Bell didn't know I existed until a week ago. What the hell was the likes of me doing permanently etched on his skin?

"What are we going to do?" Char spoke from right next to me, and I didn't notice her move.

"Me. You mean what am I going to do, right? Not we. This is my mess, and I'll clean it up." To soften my words, I squeezed her forearm gently. My friend needed to stay as far away from me as possible. Didn't she learn her lesson when she almost drowned because of my stupidity?

"Oh, you better believe it's we. They attacked me today, too. It's personal now." Char narrowed her gaze on me, her lips pressed so hard they turned white at the edges.

"Char, please. I'm begging you," I pleaded with my friend, although I knew it was useless. When she made up her mind, there was no convincing her otherwise. "This is my problem, and I'll never forgive myself if something happens to you. Please."

"And what? I should just go on with my life while they are threatening you and trying to kill you?" Huffing in indignation, she shoved my shoulder jokingly. "I think not. They want to play it that way, I say we bring out the big guns."

"What are you talking about?" I was honestly confused.

"You really are daft sometimes. Think, Allie." Taking hold of my shoulders with both hands, she turned me to fully face her. "They hired you because whoever it is couldn't take that book by themselves. Which means you are more powerful than them. And if Dimitri was stronger, he could've prevented you from stealing it, too. Which means all they have is threats and hired thugs to come after us."

I blinked at her.

"And you know what we have?" My eyebrows raised in question because I couldn't breathe, little less talk. Char grinned wickedly at me. "A badass witch and a badass sorceress."

I barked out a surprised laugh.

"They won't know what hit them." Char winked and dashed for her tote. "Let's move."

Chapter Thirteen

Returning to the dingy motel was like a sucker-punch to the gut. The Spanish-style building with its chipping paint, a few missing rooftiles, and a couple of letters burned out in the sign added to my gloomy mood more than it should've. Not that we couldn't afford a five-star hotel, all-inclusive and everything, but it was hard to stay under the radar when people were trying to kill you if you are bathing in luxury. Why couldn't I hide while soaking in a claw-footed tub in the Hilton presidential suite?

Hiding sucked big time.

"Stop dragging your feet, Allie. Move your butt." Char tugged on my arm enthusiastically, her bare feet slapping a staccato over the pavement. She lost her shoes in the killer wave that smacked us around, thanks to the water mage.

My thoughts drifted to the two attackers. I made them human. My heart lurched hard before it splattered at my feet. I found the spell in my mother's journal in the section she had named dark-edge magic. Blood magic. I stayed away from it and never would've touched it, but the few

Stolen Magic

pages written in her elegant swirling scroll got my attention. If I was honest with myself, I never thought it'd work. It wasn't unheard of for a powerful witch to have dampened the powers of another before. It was written in all the warnings throughout law enforcement books and military documents to forward to the MPO agenda. Even some mages could do it, from what I'd heard, but only to another with control of the same element. To take the magic for good and for a person to lose their power signature was unheard of.

So, how in the hell did I manage to do it?

The door protested loudly when Char yanked it open and shoved me inside the musty smelling room. My face scrunched when the odor of bleach, dust, and some unknown activities smacked me hard, wrinkling my nose in the process. Part of the shredded sheet we used to bandage Char's arm was spread across one of the single beds, and the chipped chair with threadbare fabric on the cushion was pushed under the bolted-to-the-floor table. Who would steal an old scratched-out table from the place was beyond me. As a thief, I took great offense to that. In fact, it was actually a personal insult.

Okay, fine. I was deflecting.

"We need to go back to our apartment," Char muttered more to herself than me while rushing around the room, collecting what little stuff we left behind in the morning, and stuffing it inside her tote. No kidding that bag was an abyss of mystery. "I need *stuff*." What she meant was, she needed ingredients for her potions and talismans.

"We were attacked twice in less than twelve hours," I pointed out in case she had forgotten our ordeal from earlier that day. "I really don't think we should go anywhere near that building." My friend turned toward me, her mouth already open to say something, but I was having none of that. "I'm not budging on this, Char. If you need something, we can grab it from the store on our way to another crappy motel just like this one. Whose to say the mages didn't follow us from the apartment to the store?"

"Right, and they waited until it was lunch time to kill us because they didn't want to interfere with us making a profit for the day, I'm sure," she snarked, the trademark glare known as "I'm a second from losing it" firmly in place. "I watched you and Dimitri while you *talked*"—I seriously didn't appreciate the way she said "talk" like she knew I dumbly thought the alpha was going to kiss me when he only hid his hand to show me his magic— "and I have a feeling those two were following him, not you. I guess they thought you were an easier target, so they sent vamps after you." My forehead puckered at her gleeful laugh.

"Thanks." My dragged out reply had her pausing her frantic collection of shirts and pants that were sprinkled around the room.

"Tell your ego to take a backseat, girl. This is a good thing, trust me." Her gaze searched my face, and I couldn't hide my doubtful expression from those laser beams of hers. "When someone is going for your head, you want them to think you are easy to kill. Otherwise, they'll send their best, and both of us would be toast right now."

I couldn't argue with that logic, so I kept my mouth shut. She was always the one seeing the bigger picture in any given situation. I was one of those who focused like a mule on one thing and couldn't see the forest from the trees because of it. Not that I'd ever admit that to anyone, including the woman in front of me.

"I know that." With an innocent shrug, I looked away from her penetrating stare. I pulled the burner phone that I used only for jobs not involving any wax, essential oils, or crystals and turned it on. "I have absolutely no issue giving that arrogant ass the book back, but the name he wants from me is a no-go. One, I never ask for a name. Two, the client is still AWOL, and even if I wanted to track him, I don't know how."

The empty screen of the phone with its weak light stared back at me like a death warrant. With my heart in my throat, I fumbled with the buttons to open the inbox, but only my own text messages glared back at me. Four texts with no reply. Whoever the person was, I knew he received the first one I sent when I told him the job was done. The money dropped in my account in less than five minutes. It was a bogus account connected to a dozen or so other accounts that bounces the amount transferring it from place to place until it was impossible for anyone to track it before it landed in my personal savings. When delivering the merchandise, I never delivered it personally or face to face. It was always dropped into a safety deposit box in any number of places, never the same, by a courier I followed to ensure no one got sticky hands. A thief never trusted easily. Me? I never trusted anyone, period. Well, apart from Char.

"I'll fix that." It took me a moment for Char's words to register, and my eyes flicked to her face. She was acting too innocent for my liking.

"What do you mean 'you'll fix that?'" My gaze narrowed on her, but she was looking at anything but me. "Charmaine Mariatti. Fix it how?"

"Stop using my full name like some prison warden, Allie. You know that never works on me." Oh, but it worked. The rounded corners of her cheekbones were turning dusky red, and her hands were fretting over the ripped sheet as if she could glue it back together. "I know someone that can at least tell us where the call was made when the person called you."

"It's a burner phone for a reason, Char. It cannot be traced." Although it warmed my heart to know she wanted to call in a favor so she could help me, I knew it was a waste of time.

"It can be traced in this instance. And if anyone can trace it, it's this guy." I perked up at that, all sorts of questions springing to the tip of my tongue, but she kept talking. "After seeing that he or she sent vamps after you but mages after Dimitri, I have a feeling he was not too careful and didn't cover his tracks with you. It'll work, you'll see."

My jaw clamped shut so hard I could hear my molars grinding. Char meant well. I knew she did. But there were only so many insults a girl could take. I was nearing my limit, and I had a feeling when I exploded all sorts of unnecessary words were going to spill that I didn't mean or want to say out loud. Or think for that matter. My problem was, when I was angry, I lashed out with the intent to hurt whoever had upset me. I regretted everything the moment the anger drained from me, which was in less than five minutes usually, but I knew I did a lot of damage in that time. I didn't mean to, but I did. I never wanted that to happen with my only friend.

Char didn't deserve it.

So, with that in mind, I bit the inside of my mouth until I tasted blood and nodded. "Okay. Let's go visit this guy and see what he can do."

"Thank you, Allie." Tears shimmered in her eyes, and she blinked fast to keep them at bay. "I promise you won't regret it."

"Why are you thanking me?" Taken aback, I even flinched like I'd never seen her before.

"For having enough trust in me to allow me to share this with someone else. I know you never do that, but I swear on my magic that I trust this guy. He will die before he says a word to anyone about it."

"Because he cares for you that much that he will die before he betrays your trust, or you care for him enough to blindly trust him?" There was no judgment in my tone, and she knew it. I just wanted to know what I was getting myself into.

"Neither." Her chin jutted out in that stubborn way it always did when she wanted to challenge me to argue with her. "He is a good man and will never do anything to hurt those he calls friends."

"Yet, I've never heard of him until now." It was just an observation, not a reprimand, and I waved my hand to usher her out of the room. "You'll tell me more about him on the way. The longer we linger here, the bigger the chances are that, if we were followed, another attack will come."

"We must stop at the store first," Char reminded me, and she didn't wait to be told twice to leave. Still barefoot, she was already out the door before she finished the sentence. "I just need a couple of things and we will be off. The guy lives in Glendale, so it'll take an hour or more with traffic to get there."

"Lead the way, friend." I was more than happy to leave the motel room behind, even though I didn't change out of the clothing that had white patches forming all over from the salty water of the ocean.

Hopefully the guy was as good as Char claimed.

Otherwise we were out of options.

Chapter Fourteen

It took almost two hours to reach Glendale since people were driving like their one mission in life was to stress me out to the point I wanted to stop the car and strangle them. Lucky for them, we stopped a passing Uber to take us part way before we switched to another in hopes to evade anyone that might be tailing us. Somewhere between Santa Monica and Glendale, I got a strong suspicion that Char was having way too much fun with the whole thing, and she was overdoing it. She even had her tote shoved in my lap over my small duffel bag, and I'd never seen her part from it outside the shop and the apartment. The way she kept glancing around, stuck close to the buildings we were passing between Ubers, and deepening her tone when giving an address was too James Bond-ish for my tastes.

"You can drop us off at the CVS parking lot," she murmured to the poor middle-aged man who did a double take in the rearview mirror when he noticed her leaning way too close to his head between the seats.

I yanked her back with a fistful of fabric.

"We would appreciate it very much." I gave the driver what I hoped was an apologetic smile, but the way he frowned told me I probably looked constipated.

My groan followed the squealing tires when the Uber fishtailed out of the parking lot around the pharmacy. I had no doubt he thought we were either on drugs—if he noticed the white patches of dried salt water on my clothing —or he thought we needed medication for mental illness— if he judged Char's exaggerated spy mood. After the last couple of hours, I was ready to reach our destination with the same enthusiasm Char had when she took over our mission.

"Well, he wasn't a talker." My friend huffed, hitching her tote higher on her shoulder. "Aren't you supposed to be a talker if you do that kind of a job? It should be in their form under the field that's required."

"I'm not sure he had time to answer any of your questions before you asked a new one, Char." I couldn't help the tilt of my lips when they stretched into a smile. "I swear you didn't take a breath the full hour the poor guy was stuck with us."

"Humph." Her nose lifted in the air, and she side-eyed me. "I'm a chatty Cathy when I'm nervous. Sue me."

That just brought home the gravity of our situation. Since I'd known her, I'd never seen Char talk so much. Lost in thought, I followed a step behind her as she led us up the street. She turned left when we reached a set of lights down Glendale Boulevard, and I stared absently at the small Italian delis, Armenian restaurants promising authentic food, and the many tobacco shops glowing bright with signs of different flavored vapes. When we reached a car wash, the blast of air from their machines yanked me out of my internal torment, and I looked around more alert.

"This is Burbank, Char. We left Glendale a block back, I think." And like an omen from the universe, a large sign came into view with the name of a sushi restaurant in Japanese characters, with Burbank written under it in bright red. I stabbed my finger at it as if I needed to prove I was correct.

The burst of air from the car wash had me jerking as if something bit me.

I glared at the building.

"I know, it's not far now." With a fast glance up and down the street, she darted across it, jaywalking the six lanes.

I rushed after her, a horn blaring behind me.

"You trying to get us killed the old-fashioned way?" I panted as I jumped on the sidewalk with the agility of a pregnant rhino. My ankle wobbled, and I almost lost my balance.

"You need to work on your stamina, Allie." She wasn't even winded, while I sounded like a freight train behind her.

We passed a bus stop with an ad for a TV show flickering on the screen, and my stomach growled when my eyes landed on the fruit stalls in front of a convenience store next to it. I had no idea when I'd eaten last, and my body was not too shy to remind me. My feet had a mind of their own, and I was halfway to the store when Char snatched me by the arm and tugged me away from it.

"We will order something while we wait for Damian to trace the call." My friend chuckled when I grumbled something about dying on an empty stomach. I was not kidding. It was eating itself ever since I noticed the delicious apples and peaches lining the stalls. "It's up here."

I followed the direction of her finger to a small house tucked between two rows of buildings. It looked unassuming, with a lawn that was a tiny patch of grass, a faded red roof, and freshly painted white walls on the outside. The one window visible from the street had a long wooden planter with a bunch of wilted flowers that were more brown than green. Char led me across the narrow path to the front door, and my feet shuffled uneasily when she knocked on it.

Silence met us.

Char rapped her knuckles two more times, each time harder than the last, and proceeded to mush the doorbell longer than was polite. It chirped and squealed until, at some point, it stuttered and died. No sound came from it the next time she jabbed her thumb on it.

"I think it's safe to say he is not home." My drawl was met with a stubborn flat line that used to be her mouth a moment before. "It's known to happen, for humans to leave their habitat." My attempt to lighten the mood didn't have the desired effect. My friend Char was a tough audience.

My shoulders jerked to my ears when she swirled around and started pounding her fist on the door. "Damian, open the god damn door or I'll break it."

Freaked out because Char was acting possessed, my head swiveled so I could see if anyone was staring at the two crazy women. I wanted to be ready to run if anyone called the cops. Last thing I needed, on top of mages and vamps coming after me, was the police.

"Char, we can come—"

The door cracked open a sliver, cutting off my protest. Although the sun was blasting outside, it was pitch black inside the house, which made it difficult to see who was behind the slightly ajar front door. It stayed like that a long second before it swung open, and Char stormed inside like her tail was on fire. With a gasp, I dashed after her. I had no idea who this Damian character was, so I wanted to be close if he attacked her. If anyone tried to break my front door with their fists and killed my doorbell, I'd attack them for sure.

"Char, darling. What a pleasant surprise," came a smooth, husky drawl from my left, and like an idiot, I jumped away from it.

There was a dim light coming from what I assumed was a lamp but later found out was some sort of a plant I'd never seen before. The low glow cast shadows over the sharp planes of the man's face, turning what I guessed was handsome into something sinister and straight out of a Dracula movie. My magic churned at the center of my chest, readying to blast him if he so much as twitched in our direction. One look at the lit-up vegetation told me everything I needed to know about our host-slash-hacker.

"Char, I thought your friend was a human." The accusation was clear in the tone of my voice.

"You assumed he was a human," Char huffed while Damian's grin grew as if it pleased him that he'd surprised me. "I never said he was."

"And you brought a friend. How delightful," the man in question purred as if pleased at hearing the tone of his voice.

"If I blast your arroga—"

"Allie, no." Char didn't let me finish my threat before jumping between us with her arms raised like a basketball player. "He is a pro at getting on your nerves, but he does that when he doesn't trust people. The same way you act all uppity when you don't know someone. I swear, he is not an asswipe."

I squinted my displeasure at her.

"Damian, this is Alaska. My best friend. I've told you about her." She spoke to him but didn't look away from me.

"My apologies, Alaska." The change in tone and attitude gave me whiplash. I craned my head sideways to give Damian a better look around Char. "I don't like surprise visits if I don't expect people." His glare was aimed at the back of my friend's head.

"Damian, we need your help." Char's words had him stiffening, and the glare was replaced by genuine worry. She turned to face him, and I gaped while he worriedly searched her face. "We need you to track a call made on a burner phone. If you can't, the chances are Allie and I might get killed after tomorrow midnight."

I gasped right along with Damian.

"Me. *I* might die." For some reason, I felt compelled to soothe the horror written all over his face. It would be obvious to a blind person that he cared for her.

"We will both die if it comes to that," Char told him calmly as if we were discussing the weather. Damian was already moving deep into the house, calling us to follow with a flick of his fingers over his shoulder.

That was how we ended up with a Druid helping us stay alive.

Chapter Fifteen

"I didn't think there were any Druids in LA." I stared at the line of monitors spread around a tall gamer's chair, and the entirety of Damian's basement reminded me of some scene from the Matrix.

"There are none." The pointed look he gave me over his shoulder drilled his meaning into my brain until I gave him a cautious nod in return.

"Right." Swallowing thickly, I dared a glance at Char, but she was staring at her twisting fingers.

Damian stretched his arm in my direction and opened his hand palm up, though he didn't turn his head from the monitors, the fingers from his other flying over the keys of the keyboard. With a shaking hand, I dropped the burner phone in his outstretched palm and sucked in a breath when he snatched it like a fly trap.

According to MPO, there were only a handful of Druids left in the world. Long lived, they were the loners of the supernatural world and didn't mingle with anyone but others of their kind, and they all needed to be surrounded by nature so they could maintain their powers. Earth magic was their specialty, and from what little I'd read about them, they could wield it so well that it could be used to battle anyone, no matter how powerful they were. Druids were revered for their ability to open portals between realms as well as anywhere in the world. Which, thanks to power-hungry monsters who used to capture them to use them for notorious purposes, was the main reason most of them were dead. That's why they hid and never announced themselves to anyone.

How did Char become a friend with one in the middle of a metropolis?

"This might take a while," Damian said while his fingers danced over the keys. My burner phone was plugged into a tower that was placed close to his thigh, a cord curling between them. "You might want to take a seat."

Without a word, I looked around and shuffled to the corner of the room where a plastic chair was wedged between some boxes. Char moved to a wingback chair opposite me and plopped on it with a sigh. She still refused to meet my eyes.

Curiosity got the better of me.

"How do you two know each other?" Damian's fingers paused over the keyboard, and Char's head ducked so low she almost folded in half.

"Damian is one of the suppliers we order herbs from for our store," my friend said woodenly from behind the curtain of her hair. If I didn't have a hairline, I had no doubt my eyebrows would've crawled all the way to the back of my head. "He's been supplying us with them for a little over a year."

"Oh." My eloquent reply had Char flinching.

I shouldn't have been upset that she never mentioned

him, but I was. It smarted something fierce, and not because she'd met a guy and never shared it with me. It was because he was a Druid, something I'd think anyone would be excited to share with a best friend. Almost like seeing a unicorn. Keeping Damian's identity a secret had been a safe bet for Char, though. The same way she kept mine hidden because, for all intents and purposes, until Dimitri Bell barged into my life, I was one of the unicorns, too.

Damian muttered something under his breath that I missed, so I tucked my hands under my thighs and leaned forward on the chair. "I'm sorry, what?"

"It's like this person isn't even trying." The Druid chuckled, lifting one hand to rub the back of his neck.

His dirty blond hair was cut short with the top left longer, the strands curling over the tops of his ears. Unlike the alpha, Damian, although similar in height, he had more of an athletic physique, all lean muscle and wiry frame, which was characteristic to his kind. Something I'd missed but had become obvious when his arm lifted, and the long-sleeved shirt crawled up his forearm to reveal the glowing swirls on his skin—another dead giveaway of what he was and why he was wearing long sleeves in summer in the middle of LA. I assumed the dead flowers on the outside of the house were a camouflage to hide what he was. Clever, but …

It must be killing him to see them daily. There was no doubt in my mind about that.

"Ummm." The hum coming from the Druid didn't sound too promising.

"Something wrong?" After his last comment, a small amount of hope had bloomed inside me, and I had thought maybe I had misjudged Char. Perhaps there was a way to give the shifter what he wanted so he would leave me be.

The uncertain humming splashed that whole idea with cold water, and I sagged in the plastic chair, holding my breath.

"No, nothing wrong but this cannot be right." Damian spoke under his breath while numbers and letters flickered and moved across the screens. "I could've followed the wrong trail. One moment."

Char and I looked at each other and stood, crowding behind the Druid as if what he was looking at made any sense to either of us. Patience had never been my virtue, so I nibbled on my lower lip and raked the outer seam of my pants with the fingernail of my forefinger. I didn't realize I was making a sound until Char's hand closed over mine and stopped my scraping. I gave her a sheepish smile. The wait, now that I knew Damian had something, was nerve-wracking.

"Well, I would say the two of you have a big problem, indeed." The Druid removed his fingers from the keyboard and leaned back in his chair. He glanced at both of us in turn with a troubled expression on his face, and dread pooled in the pit of my belly.

"Where did they call from?" Char was braver than me. I couldn't form words to save my life. All of a sudden, I honestly didn't want to know.

"According to the trail, which I triple checked just to be certain …" Damian blew out a heavy and loaded with worry sigh through his pursed lips. His pale green gaze, which was full of pity, landed on me, and my heart tripped over itself. I tensed as if I could escape his next words. "The call came directly from the office of the CEO of Ice Matrix CO."

"What?"

"That asswipe," Char hissed at the same time as I shouted my disbelief too loud for the not-so-large basement.

"That can't be true." The denial burst out of me, but not even I believed it.

Everything replayed in my mind in a loop. Me stealing the book, and the person walking in just after I opened the safe through a door that wasn't supposed to be visible to anyone from the outside, only to whoever had it locked in that room. The flowers I received with the threatening note. The stairway where somehow Dimitri just happened to bring his wife to be right when I was in his building. The vampire attack right after it. The alpha walking into my store demanding we talk at the pier, and the perfectly timed attack by the mages. His rescue while he stayed out of the fight, leaving me to battle the elementals so I could reveal my deepest, darkest secret.

I didn't realize I was shaking and whimpering until Damian jumped from the chair in alarm and Char wrapped me in a hug. I could see their lips moving, but the sound of my thundering heart was too loud in my ears, and I couldn't hear anything apart from it. My breathing was too fast, and I struggled to fill my lungs with air, which made dark spots dance in the corners of my eyes. In the middle of all that, I couldn't feel anything. My body was cold and numb, and Char's hug was like hugging a stone since I couldn't sense her wrapped around me at all.

Damian locked his gaze on my wide one, and his irises started to glow, low at first but brightening by the second. Everything else around me vanished, giving me tunnel vision where only two green glowing orbs became my entire focus. My friend was the only thing keeping me standing because my knees gave out, and I sagged in her hold. Somewhere in the back of my mind I was aware that I was having a panic attack, but there was nothing I could do to stop it.

Stolen Magic

It started like a tiny warm spot in my sternum. I startled from the sensation, worried that my magic was gathering because of my fear and would unleash at any moment, destroying everything and everyone around me. When it spread over my torso like a balm, I took a stuttering breath, realizing it wasn't my power at all. The Druid was doing something to calm me, and to my surprise, I didn't fight him. In fact, I added whatever little magic I could to aid him, and soon the basement came into view. Our eyes stayed locked until I was able to hear their voices.

"Deep breaths, Allie. I got you, girl. Please," Char choked through a tearful tone. "Slow, deep breaths, sync them with mine." She blew out air that ruffled strands of my hair around the side of my face.

I followed directions mechanically, too afraid to return to the numb state.

"I'll be right back." Damian, his face blanched of all color, darted out of the basement.

We stayed breathing in sync where we stood, and he was back in less than a minute. A mug was clutched in his fingers, the liquid in it rippling from the tremor in his hand. The Druid took my hand and curled it around the drink before bringing it to my lips. I stared at his face unblinking.

"It's tea," he assured me as he pressed the rim to my mouth. "It'll help calm you down, nothing else. I swear it on my life."

"Drink, Allie. Please." The way Char's voice broke made me part my lips and let the Druid tip the mug up.

Bitter liquid slid down my throat, and after swallowing a large gulp, I coughed, spraying Damian's shirt with it. If I expected him to flinch, I would've been disappointed. He stood steady and composed, lifting the tea to dribble in my mouth again. His gaze never left my face.

"Enough." After half of the mug was empty, I turned my face away. "I just need to sit."

Char shuffled in a half circle, while Damian turned his chair and they lowered me on it. My friend kneeled at my side, turning her face up to look at me, and the Druid leaned back to perch on the desk next to his keyboard. With all my senses returning, so did the familiar anger that thawed the residual ice that tightened my veins.

"He set me up," I told Char through tingling lips.

From the corner of my vision, I noticed Damian frowning at me. He never asked any questions about why we needed the call traced or anything else. All the Druid knew was that our lives were in danger, and we needed to know where a call came from on the burner phone. Idly, I wondered how the Druid managed to trace it, but it was a distant and a momentarily fleeting thought.

"He fooled me too, Allie." Char beseeched me to stay calm with her gaze. "I believed he was sincerely asking who wanted to steal from him, as well."

Damian again surprised us by not asking any questions.

The anger finally brought me back to myself, and I clenched my teeth. "If Dimitri Bell thinks I'm going down without a fight, he has another thing coming."

"Didn't he just become a member of MPO?" The first question Damian uttered was like a bucket of cold water dousing my rage.

And just like that, any hope I had of staying alive died.

Chapter Sixteen

Damian sent us on our way with a demand that Char call him as soon as we found a motel. He gave her a phone, one that definitely couldn't be traced according to the Druid, and a wad of cash he pulled out from under the desk in the basement. Our stealthy way of sneaking around turned out to be incredibly dumb since we'd used a credit card to book the motel room. I had no idea why we didn't think of it, but there it was.

On wooden legs, I walked to the narrow bed on the right in yet another dingy room and plopped on the edge with a grunt. The duffel dropped at my feet with a heavy thump. On a good note, there were no extra odors in this one apart from bleach and laundry detergent. One of the walls, however, had a yellowish stain of an unidentifiable nature, and the mud brown carpet had a few rips fraying like sprouting grass on the floor. The second narrow bed had a bare mattress with linen dumped in a pile on top of it. Char busied herself with that while I watched her dispassionately.

"I'm sorry." Her head snapped up when I muttered my apology.

"Why are you sorry exactly?" A line formed between her perfectly shaped eyebrows. I could see the strain and stress at the lines, which were more prominent on the outside corners of her eyes.

"For getting upset with you every time you called me daft, to start with." Scrubbing a hand over my face, I sighed. "All of it makes sense, you know."

"That you are daft?" I could tell she was worried that I'd lost my mind.

"That too, but I was talking about Dimitri. Now that I go back to that night when I stole the cursed book, it makes perfect sense, actually."

"How so?" Forgetting the linens she was tugging over the mattress, she sat with one leg curled under her, leaning one arm on the still-unmade bed.

"A week before he made that call, he was accepted as an honorary member of the MPO." Char's eyes widened when she caught the direction of my thoughts. "What better way to show your worth than killing a witch in the first month of your membership? Well, he could've done it in a week, but I have a feeling he is toying with me."

My friend was grinding her teeth.

"Both attacks were just added proof he needed that I was indeed what he claimed me to be. And like an idiot, I didn't just confirm that I was a witch in plain sight, I actually did a spell only a handful of witches from the olden days were capable of performing."

"I always told you that you are more powerful than you think you are." A sad smile curled her lips. "He is not going to win this, Allie." My breath caught at the determination brightening her dark eyes. "I won't let him."

"It's a battle I don't think we can win, Char. MPO wiped almost all of the witches from the face of the earth. What can one witch do against them?"

"You assume he announced his plans to his new buddies, my friend." Doubt was evident on her face, but she kept going. "Dimitri is too arrogant to share anything. He would want to kill you first before parading you around like a poached kill in front of everyone."

"You and the alpha are that close you know how his mind works?" My jab had the desired effect. She snorted.

"I know his kind."

"Apparently you know many kinds I wasn't aware of."

"I deserve that." With a sigh, she jerked back, hitting the mattress hard and throwing an arm over her face so I couldn't see her. The dusky red of her blush was visible, however. "It's not that I didn't want to tell you because he is a Druid, you know."

"You don't have to tell me now either, Char. Your life is your own, regardless of the fact that we are best friends." I liked talking about her instead of my upcoming death, but I didn't want her to feel like she was obligated to tell me everything. I lied to her about a job, for goodness sake. I had no right to demand any honesty from her.

"And this is why I tell you that you are daft, Allie." Forgetting about her embarrassment, Char propped up on her elbows. "Me not telling you about Damian had nothing to do with you and everything to do with me."

"You are half Druid?" I squeaked, gaping at her.

"What?" Char laughed so hard that tears gathered in the corners of her eyes. "No." Gasping for air, she rolled on the bed.

I glared. There was nothing funny about what I'd asked.

"I'm not half Druid, I swear. One hundred percent

sorceress right here." Wiping her eyes with the back of her hand, she sat up, and all the humor drained from her face. "I never mentioned him to you because if I did, it would mean I acknowledged my attraction to him. Actually, until this very moment, I was doing great living in denial. Now it's out in the universe since I said it out loud." Her mouth twisted into a grimace.

"Is he a psycho?" I leaned forward, draping my forearms over my knees. "Because, let me tell you this. If he is some stalker dude, I'm going to take him down before I die, I promise you that much. Druid or not, I'll bury him next to those wilting flowers on his window."

"I love you for it, Allie, but no, he is not a psycho stalker." Tears welled in her eyes again, but her smile was bright.

"You think he doesn't like you like that?" I ducked my head to stare at her incredulously. "The guy was practically salivating the moment he saw you, Char. A blind person could see it." The longer I thought about it, the more the idea of the two of them seemed appealing. If I was going to be killed, at least Char wouldn't be alone.

She'd need someone after I died.

I knew she wouldn't be able to handle it alone.

"I know he likes me like *that*." Her face bloomed with a dusky red color, making her cheeks redder than before. "The problem is, he likes a lot of women the same way. I don't like him in a way to only have a casual fling, unfortunately."

Everything she said was valid if my death was not looming over my head. Casual or not, Damian was the perfect person to be around Char if the shifter's wish came true.

"Call him to let him know where we are." My sudden lack of jabs made her suspicions spike. "You promised him, and I just remembered. I have a ton of things on my mind." The reminder of Dimitri Bell had her ruffling inside her tote in the blink of an eye.

I stretched out on the bed and stared unseeing at the ceiling while she spoke briefly to the Druid. Wanting to give my friend some space, I rolled off the mattress and went to the small bathroom, closing the door behind me. Char's voice drifted after me through the thin walls, but at least she had some semblance of privacy. I was sure I'd hear about it when I emerged, but I was fine with that.

The woman staring back at me from the cracked mirror above the sink didn't look familiar at all. The diagonal line split my reflection in two, distorting it enough to change my features. One thing that was the same was the defeated look in my eyes. Even my irises seemed strange, a paler green somehow. My hair was dull and plastered around my head in matted clumps. The ocean water hadn't done me any favors, and for a moment, I wondered what the Druid had thought when I'd stepped inside his home like this. Damian didn't even blink strangely at my appearance. Char hadn't fared much better, but if anyone could pull off an almost drowned look and make it a new thing, it was my friend. She had the ability to make a hole-ridden sack look like a Versace.

"Allie." The soft knock on the door startled me out of my thoughts. I had turned into a frightened rabbit in the last week or so, jumping at sounds constantly.

"Done?" She stepped aside when I opened the door, her blush firmly in place.

"Yeah, he said if we need anything, he is a phone call or text away." The red on her cheekbones deepened.

"Good to know, but I don't think we will need

anything." I snatched the duffel off the floor and tugged the zipper open. "I actually have a plan."

"Are you going to share, or do I need to beat it out of you." When I tried to move around her with a handful of clothes so I could take a shower and wash all the salt stuck to my skin away, she blocked my way. "You know I will."

"First, I'm going to shower so I can feel like a normal witch. You should do it too, because we look like rats after a flood. Avoid the mirror when you go inside the bathroom."

Her foot started tapping.

"Dimitri wants everything done on his time." With a sigh, I hugged the bundle of fabric closer to my chest. "Everything up to this point has had perfect timing, which tells me he has something planned right at midnight tomorrow. So, I'm going to throw him off by showing up at noon tomorrow. It's still twelve, only PM instead of AM."

"Sounds like a good idea. We will pop in at noon and play it by ear." With a firm nod, she stepped aside, but I snatched her arm and waited until she locked gazes with me.

"I will go at noon, Char. Alone." Her mouth opened, but I shook my head. "Well, alone with the book. You'll wait here or at Damian's."

"I can come with you, or I'll just follow behind you." With a twitch of her shoulder, she tugged her arm out of my grip. "It makes no difference to me. It's not like the asswipe can transport Ice Matrix CO. from the street it's on. Go ahead, try and leave me behind, I dare you."

Our staring match did nothing but start a throbbing headache behind my eyes, so I relented. After a reluctant nod of agreement, I headed for the shower that was calling my name. I had dried salt in places that never should've seen it. As much as I dreaded having water coating me again from head to toe, I was willing to endure the discomfort.

Char was silent behind me, for which I was grateful. She'd have enough time to yell and scream tomorrow after I was gone. I'd never used my powers on Char before. We made a pact to never do that to each other. I was going to go back on a promise, and I had no doubt the betrayal would hurt my friend. But I saw no other choice if I wanted to protect her.

Maybe she'd forgive me easier since I'd be dead. Either way, I was firmly set in my decision.

I was leaving Char, fast asleep, behind.

Chapter Seventeen

A blurry eyed sorceress met my gaze early the next morning. Char must've had a shower sometime after I fell asleep because I didn't hear her, but the evidence of it was in the frizzy tendrils of her curly hair that had escaped her loosely wrapped bun. Dark smudges slashed crescents under her eyes, and her cheeks seemed sunken. Gone was the usual floor-length dress that was her go-to in terms of her personal fashion style, and in its place she wore blue jeans and a black t-shirt with "History of magic" written on it in bright orange print. I also didn't miss the stubborn jutting of her chin while she eyed me warily.

"You're up bright and early." The sun was not up yet, and the harsh yellow light from outside was peeking through the slightly parted curtain of the only window in the room.

"You know me, I'm one of those morning people." There was a rasp in her tone that told me she had not slept at all. Not that it was hard to guess, by any means.

"Demons." My hiss made her crack a fleeting smile. "I could kill for a cup of coffee."

"Ask and ye shall receive." My friend walked stiffly to the small table serving as a TV stand and plucked one cup from the cardboard tray I hadn't noticed until that moment.

As soon as I had the coffee in my hands, the roof of my mouth blistered from the large gulp I sucked through the sippy lid, but I relished the burn. The bitter taste fired up all my senses as well as my sluggish brain, and the room came fully into view. Char must've left the bathroom door open because light spilled from the one lightbulb through the crack. I stared at the line it formed on the frayed carpet while sipping the coffee cradled between both of my hands like something precious.

"I love you." My sigh sounded wistful.

Char jerked in surprise but managed a murmur. "Love you too, Allie."

"I was talking to the coffee, but I do love you as well, Char. Like, you are second on my list of 'things I love.'"

"I'm not a thing." Her glare was exaggerated, and we both snickered, although without too much joy.

It was difficult to find any semblance of normality when stress was draining both of us like leeches. I was sure, even with the couple of hours of fitful sleep I got, I didn't look any better than Char did. We stayed silent until the tray was full of empty cups. There wasn't much either of us could say, yet the air in the room was oppressive and heavy with unspoken words. I couldn't take it anymore. Neither the silence, nor my best friend avoiding eye contact.

"I think I should go alone, Char." Her loose bun unraveled from how hard she shook her head before I finished the sentence. "From what we've seen so far, Dimitri is calculating and anal for everything happening on his time. The guy takes organization skills to a whole new level, don't you think? This will throw him for a loop. I honestly don't see him reacting badly. Not while I'm in his office, anyway."

"That's too many what-if's more than I'm comfortable with." Fiddling with her hair, she kept her gaze on the floor. "You'll be alone inside that building while everyone there is on his payroll. I'm not liking the odds of that."

"There will be humans inside it, too. I really don't think he will make a scene. Last thing Ice Matrix CO. needs is a spectacle in their headquarters. Can you imagine the headlines if magic starts flying all over the place?" Halfway through my tirade, I'd begun nibbling on the side of my thumb, so I lowered my hand and curled it into a fist when I caught what I was doing. "It's not like I want to face the shifter alone. But I'm also not walking in unarmed."

"I just have a bad feeling about it, Allie." Finally, she stopped trying to wrap the thick mess of her hair and yanked the elastic band off it with a huff. "Everything we talked about makes perfect sense, and yesterday I totally agreed with it. Now …" Shuffling closer, she moved my feet to the side and sat on the bed where I was still stretched out. "Now, I'm not that convinced. Something is nagging at me that we are missing the bigger picture here."

"There is only one way to find out." I had to lower my hand again. I had no idea when I started the habit of chewing on my nails, but there it was. Cannibalism at its finest.

"I have a plan, though." Peering at me through her lashes, Char was rasping her teeth over her lower lip. Her anxiety was not helping mine one bit. "I know we have this pact where we don't ask each other anything about our powers, but—"

"But?" I prompted when she didn't continue.

"Maybe you can do whatever you do when you are on a

job to me?" It came out as something between a statement and a question. Her inflection rose slightly at the end, showcasing her uncertainty.

"I don't understand."

"Until now, no one has seen the White Kalla. She was a ghost." Her gaze seared mine, and my heart picked up speed. "Whatever magic you use on yourself, I'd like you to use it on me. That way, you will be alone as far as anyone in that building is concerned, but I'll be right next to you."

"The reason I am in this mess is because that jerk can see through my spell, Char. Did you forget that little detail?"

"Very true, but only he can see it." I thought she would be discouraged when I pointed out the facts, but instead, my friend became more animated. "As long as I'm in that building, close enough to rush to your aid if you need it, I'm good. I'll even stay in the bathrooms the whole time if you want."

"Okay, I'll bite. Let's say you are there, and he does attack." Waiting long enough for her to understand how serious I was, I continued after a long sigh. "We are no match for Dimitri Bell, Char. We are both toasts, or dog chow, whatever tickles your fancy."

"And that's where you are wrong." Her arms folded across her chest, and she squared her shoulders. "Alone, we may not be a match for the alpha. Together, we will wax all the fur from that wolf while he begs for mercy."

I barked out a surprised laugh, and she giggled. "Wax his fur? Really?" Chortling, I shook my head at her pleased grin.

"You are laughing, aren't you?"

"It might be the last time I do, so I'm going to take full advantage of it while I can." I regretted the words as soon as they left my mouth.

"So not funny."

"I didn't think it was." A long breath whistled through my pursed lips, and I nudged her away so I could swing my legs off the bed. "Let me jump in the shower so I can be ready when the time comes. We will have an early lunch before I have to face the shifter. I have less of an attitude on a full stomach. Who knows, maybe if I keep my mouth shut and don't snark, he will decide having me around the city is not that bad of an idea?"

Char said nothing, so I dragged myself to the bathroom. Avoiding the cracked mirror the best I could, I peeled off my sweats first, then my t-shirt with "I can drive a stick" and a broom printed on it off my body, as the small space fogged up with steam. The water pelted my skin and, leaning on the tiles with both palms pressed on them, I let my head hang down to my chest. My heartbeat was galloping between my ribs, so I took slow, measured breaths until I calmed it. It was beyond my power to turn back time and decline the job I'd stupidly accepted. Things were out of my control, and all I could do was go with the flow. If that stream took me to a tête-à-tête with the reaper, well ...

So, be it.

When the water turned off and my fingers were wrapped around the plastic curtain that was slightly moldy at the corners, a shriek burst out of me when the door of the bathroom banged open. Forgetting all about the disgusting mold, I clutched it to my chest so I could cover all the important bits of my anatomy. Char sashayed inside with her arms full of makeup, a hair dryer, and a bunch of brushes like I was not standing there naked.

"Umm, what happened to knocking?" I quipped cautiously. "Last time I checked, it was still acceptable behavior in modern society."

"You have nothing I don't." She dumped everything she was holding on the floor and crouched over it. Lifting her face, she narrowed her eyes on me. "You didn't grow a third nipple or a peen without telling me, did you?"

"What? No." My automatic reply only succeeded in frustrating me more. "I need to get dressed, Char. Do you mind?"

"Aha!" My friend jumped to her feet and darted out of the bathroom.

My toes had barely touched the tiles under the tub when she returned, and I had to jump back behind the moldy plastic. I had no doubt that steam was coming out of my ears.

"Ta-da," Char announced, elaborately flinging her arm to the side with a hanger in her hand so I could see what was draped on it.

"What's that?" The outfit was something I purchased for a Halloween party a few years back when I decided I could pull off a supervillain like a pro. The crossover jacket worn with nothing underneath it and the too-tight leather pants, both in dark green, were definitely not something I had in my duffel bag. I was sure of it. "I'm not wearing that."

"Yes, you are, unless you are planning on going naked." Tilting her head to the side, she smirked at me." That will do the trick, too."

"I'm not a monkey to do tricks, and I'm not wearing that." Ready to cross both arms over my chest, I almost dropped the curtain. It took a bit of fumbling and a few choice words, but my virtue stayed protected from the mean woman grinning at me. "Why do I have to wear that?"

"I'm going to do your hair and your makeup, too." Ignoring my question, she pointed at the mess on the floor.

I eyed it warily. "Why?" I whined like a petulant child.

"Because we want to unsettle him while playing his game." Char spoke conspiratorially. "But no one said we have to play fair. Dimitri Bell is an asswipe, and powerful at that, but he is still just a man. No hot-blooded testosterone-driven creature can resist a redhead dressed in leather. Trust me, the alpha won't know what hit him."

Chapter Eighteen

"I feel like an idiot," I muttered to Char, who was standing next to me in front of the Ice Matrix CO. building while she enjoyed being invisible a little too much.

While I suffered her makeover talents, my friend told me she'd been busy overnight. So she didn't wake me up, Char spent the night in the bathroom of the motel room and crafted enough potions to bring Pentagon down. All of them were stacked inside the tote draped over her shoulder, along with the cursed book that belonged to the alpha, and I twitched whenever the sound of clinking glass resonated in the space between us.

I had to admit, albeit begrudgingly, that it was a very good idea to have Char nearby with the object. It was as good of leverage as any, I supposed, and something I could hold over Dimitri Bell's head.

"You are one hot mama, Allie." Char bumped her shoulder off mine and craned her neck to stare as high as she could up the building. "I never understood why a security company needed a skyscraper."

"It's all about power and prestige. If you don't flaunt it, you don't have it, at least with these people." Something the two of us learned to hide more than anything. We both had solid chunks of money stashed away, me from jobs and Char from what I thought were rare potions sold in the store, but it turned out my friend dabbled in the black market for her savings. The way we lived, I was sure people thought we were paycheck-to-paycheck people.

Which was safe.

Had I known I didn't have long to live and wouldn't need a retirement plan, I would've had hot guys in Speedos feeding me grapes and fanning me with palm leaves while I lounged at the Bahamas. Hindsight was always twenty-twenty.

The two muscular shifters ignored me from their posts on both sides of the sliding glass doors. Squinting—a bad habit of mine since I had perfect sight—I checked if they were the same men from my previous visit, but I couldn't be sure. This time around, both had mirrored aviator glasses perched on the bridges of their noses, so it was hard to know where they were looking, too. Their faces were pointed straight ahead of them, however.

Self-consciously, I tugged my jacket down unnecessarily and squared my shoulders. With my head held high, I strode toward the sliding doors and released the breath I was holding, but only after I entered the building. Chilled air slapped me across the face and ruffled my perfectly styled red beach waves, courtesy of the sorceress next to me. My invisibility spell kept her hidden, but she wasn't allowed to talk. One word and we would be busted immediately if anyone heard her. Supernaturals, as well as humans, didn't appreciate anyone poking their noses in their business when they could see them. I really didn't want to test that theory and see what would happen when they couldn't see the person sneaking up on them.

My heart stuttered when I saw Pura behind the receptionist desk, her narrow face half hidden by the large frame of the prescription glasses she had on. Forehead puckering, I wondered why a supe would need glasses, but her head turned and all thought about it vanished when our gazes met across the vast expanse of the space. Her hair was in a tight bun at the nape of her skull, and an antique broach held the ruffled high collar of her pristine white shirt together.

"Here goes nothing," I told Char through unmoving lips before striding straight toward the older woman.

What were the odds that I'd be saved again from her by Dimitri's father? Zero, that was what. The nicer, older version of the alpha was definitely not hanging around just to come to my rescue, I was on my own.

"Hello, Pura." Going for familiarity might help ease my way to the higher levels, so I smiled at the lady. "I don't know if you remember me, but I came here the other day for an interview." Her eyelids lowered, and her piercing gaze bore into mine. "Mr. Bell senior escorted me to the office above?"

"I remember you." There was no smile, no niceties, just a flat tone to her voice.

I fidgeted where I stood, and my nervous chuckle didn't help any. My eyes widened when Char pinched my side hard, and it took everything in me not to smack her. The spot would bruise in five minutes, I was sure of it.

"I had to come for one more meeting." Praying that Pura would just leave it at that and allow me to go on my way was a little too much to ask. I hoped I wouldn't need to mention Dimitri, but it looked like I might not have a choice.

"With?" One of the older woman's eyebrows arched like she didn't believe anyone in the building would want to see me twice. I did look like a stand-in from a movie shoot, but she didn't need to give me a once over that told me she found me lacking.

I looked hot in the leather, damn it.

"Dimitri Bell." The second I dropped the alpha's name, her entire disposition changed.

"Please take a seat and I will notify Mr. Bell that you are here, Miss ..." With a pleasant smile, she waited patiently, while I had to blink a few times to assure myself I didn't imagine the previous five minutes.

"McCullough, Alaska McCullough," I mumbled and really wanted to slap myself for doing a tacky impersonation of James Bond. Char was getting inside my head with all her spy insanity.

The sorceress in question snorted softly from somewhere behind me.

"Take a seat right there, Miss McCullough." Raising slightly off her chair, Pura pointed with an open palm at the couple of armchairs clustered a few feet in front of her desk. "I will personally take you to Mr. Bell's office as soon as I announce your arrival."

Dazed, I walked to where she sent me and dropped into one of the chairs. The leather pants protested loudly, but I ignored the squeaky sound. It was summer in LA, so the damn things were glued to my legs already anyway. As Char loved to remind me, there was no beauty without pain or discomfort. Subtly I glanced at my friend and nearly laughed when I saw her twirling her forefinger around her temple and pointing to Pura.

Crossing one leg over the other with another squeak, I angled my body so the older woman couldn't see my face. "What on earth was that?" I whispered to Char.

My friend didn't have a chance to answer because I heard the putter of hurried steps coming my way. The next moment, Pura loomed over me, smiling like I'd just saved her puppy from a certain death. It was creepy to see.

"I will take you to Mr. Bell now." Her right arm swirled with flourish toward the silver doors of the elevators. I noticed she was wearing pants instead of a skirt as I suspected while the desk hid half of her body, and for some reason, I found that very suspicious. Pura seemed at that age when women, human or supernatural, preferred a skirt when wearing a suit over pants. The fact unsettled me more than it should've. Or maybe I was deflecting.

"Follow me."

The elevator arrived a lot sooner than I wanted, and we shuffled inside the small, mirrored space. Char darted right after me before the doors closed in her face. As soon as the loud ping sounded, my stomach dipped when we lurched upward. Nose twitching, I tried hard not to sneeze while I sniffed subtly and caught a familiar scent. Try as I might, I couldn't place it, but it nagged at me until we reached the floor and spilled out of the elevator.

An elegant desk with a leather chair, a landline phone, and a closed laptop was placed to the side of a double-sized black door. Instead of wood, the door was padded in a similar fashion to Char's bedframe—the one she bought a year before. There was no secretary or assistant occupying the comfortable-looking chair. A tall fern hugged one corner, and an abstract statue decorated one side table next to a long corner lounge. Apart from the blue and gray rug and a few modern paintings, the place was almost empty of anything else. Tall floor-to-ceiling windows with a full view of downtown LA made up for it.

"He is expecting you." Pura yanked me out of my perusal. My mouth opened so I could thank her, but she was already heading back inside the elevator, the door sliding shut behind her.

"I'll be here," Char whispered so softly I barely heard her. "You got this, Allie. Go tell him where to shove his threats. If you are not out in ten minutes, I'm coming in. Or just scream from the top of your lungs and I'll bust that door open."

I believed her.

The ancestors knew she had enough arsenal in that tote to bring the building, along with half of downtown, on top of our heads. With a firm bob of my head, I strode to the padded black door and gripped the golden door handle in a sweaty palm. Char offered a reassuring nod when I glanced one last time over my shoulder, and I stiffened my spine.

I pushed the door open and walked in.

Chapter Nineteen

"Miss McCullough, what a pleasant—" Dimitri's dry tone cut off and he choked on air when I waltzed inside his office like I owned the place.

His silver blue gaze smoldered and roved over me from head to toe, but a number of things became obvious to me in that same moment. One, Char had really done magic with her makeover skills judging by the reaction from the alpha. Two, I realized why the scent in the elevator was familiar. Angela was perched on a chair in front of Dimitri, the humongous oak desk the only thing separating them. Three, Pura did not announce my arrival to her boss. He was as shocked to see me standing in his office as his fiancée was.

The word left a bitter taste in my mouth.

My pulse thundered in my ears.

"I'm sorry," I stuttered stupidly. "I didn't mean to interrupt. I can wait." My fingers twitched with the need to wrap around the hilts of my daggers for some reason. I resisted, but it was a close call. What I really wanted to know was, why Pura dumped me without telling Dimitri first, but I had more important things to worry about first.

Internally, I knew I should turn and leave, but the soles of my boots were glued to the Persian rug under my feet. Also, the shifter held me prisoner with his intense stare, and all I could do was breathe and look back at him. The office around me faded into nothingness, leaving me with only the sound of my heartbeat mixed with the palpable hunger radiating from Dimitri as company.

"Aren't you going to introduce us, darling?" Angela cleared her throat and glared daggers at Dimitri.

Everything snapped into focus again, and I took a step back.

"I will see you later this evening, Angela." Rudely ignoring her request, he stepped around the desk and lifted her off the chair with a firm grip on her upper arm. "I have work to do."

And people to kill, I wanted to add, but I didn't.

What an ass.

"I can find my way out," the blonde bombshell hissed and yanked her arm out of his hold.

Dressed in a black skintight dress that barely covered the creases of her behind, she jutted her chin up and narrowed her eyes on me. Since I wasn't very tall, it was easy for people to stare down their nose at me. It never bothered me as much as seeing Dimitri's fiancée doing it.

My jaw clenched, and I kept my eyes on the alpha.

Silence stretched between the three of us. With an indignant huff, Angela snatched a clutch I didn't notice until that moment from the top of the desk and glided out of the office like a gazelle. Her hate-filled glare stayed on my face until the door slammed behind her. Her dramatic exit would've had more of a punch if the door was not padded, but the sentiment was not lost on me. She hated that I was present in the room with her man.

I hated it more, not that I could tell her.

Actually, I didn't mind it in many ways if I was honest with myself. I very much liked looking at the too-handsome-for-his-own-good shifter, with his high cheekbones, full lips, and a body out of every woman's wet dream. It was his murderous attempts on my life that rubbed me wrong. With that thought, anger surged to the forefront of my mind.

"Trouble in paradise already?" Cocking my hip, I planted my hand on it for good measure, and to hide the tremor in my fingers. His gaze tracked every move I made like a hawk. "I did offer to make you a candle. It still stands, since it's obvious you need it."

"Miss McCullough, please." His large hand pointed at the chair that Angela had been using a moment before. "Take a seat."

I waited until he moved around the desk and faced me—okay, I totally checked out his firm, rounded backside the whole time—to present him with my smug grin. My expression formed a line between his brows, and when his head tilted to the side, a lock of dark hair fell across his forehead. It was my turn to follow the direction of his strong fingers as he brushed it aside.

"I prefer to stand, thank you." My reply came out jumbled when a knowing glint entered his irises.

"What brings you here so early?" Unperturbed, he lowered the part of his body I admired the most to the leather executive chair. Forearms pressed on the desk, Dimitri laced his fingers and peered at me through lashes that belonged on a woman, not a brute like himself. Thick and slightly curled, they made his silver blue eyes pop in contrast to the tanned skin on his face.

"I'm here to tell you that I'm no longer playing your game." When he said nothing and continued to gaze at me with an unreadable expression on his face, I fought the need to fidget. "I figured out everything, and I came to tell you that you can take the book and get the hell out of my life." Tugging the said object I threw it on his desk and watched it slide over the wood until it bumped his arm.

If I wasn't staring at him the way I was, I would've missed the subtle stiffening of his shoulders. The fabric of the dark gray shirt hugging his torso crinkled across his bulging biceps and chest. "Is that so?" The Russian accent became thicker than usual. "You figured me all out. Well done, Miss McCullough. Care to share your findings with me?" Snatching the small book he dumped it in the first drawer on his right without taking his eyes off of me.

Anger prickled my skin, and I felt heat spread from my chest up my neck and all the way to the tips of my ears. Leaning forward, I bared my teeth at him and spoke in a hiss. "I know you made the call to hire me for the job, Dimitri. I traced the call to this very office. If I am a thief, so are you now. So, let's cut the crap and be honest for once, huh? Who said there was no honor among thieves?"

My temper always got the best of me. Had I not been so consumed with outrage, I would've noticed when the color drained from his face. Or the way his entire body turned from flesh and blood to a marble statue, unnaturally still. It wasn't until he jumped to his feet and sent his chair crashing against the wall behind him that I came out of my tirade and gasped. Expecting him to attack me, my knees bent, and I snatched the daggers I had sheathed around my thighs.

"Take it easy, Miss McCullough." He held his hands to his sides, his palms facing the desk. "I assure you I have not hired you or anyone else to steal my mother's family journal full of spells."

My eyes nearly popped out of my skull when he spoke freely about witch magic in the middle of the building where anyone could hear him. It must all be a trick, I decided. Bell was trying to get me to talk about what I am. Panic gripped me, and he must've noticed because he tried coming toward me around the desk before he thought better of it.

"My office is soundproofed against supernatural hearing." Satisfying my curiosity, he pointed at the padded door. So, that's why it looked weird? Who knew?

"If you expect me to believe it wasn't you, you must really think I'm dumb." My feet slid closer to the door by an inch. Dimitri didn't miss the movement. "I know your type. Those like you don't give free access to what they consider theirs, be it a person or an office. The call was made from that phone." My dagger stabbed the air toward the rectangular phone at the corner of his desk.

For the first time, and that included the time he stood only wrapped in a silky sarong in the middle of my store, Dimitri seemed troubled. More than troubled, the alpha looked almost afraid. It doused my anger long enough to notice the change in his posture. It was almost as if he was holding back from snatching me and making a run for it.

He raked his fingers over the top of his head, grabbing a fistful of hair and messing it up. "I took over the family business when I returned to America from Russia. I'm not sure how aware you are of what transpired with the transfer." A sigh passed his kissable lips, and he stared unseeing through the floor-to-ceiling windows stretching the expanse of one wall of the large office. "It was not pretty, as you Americans like to say. My father did not relish giving up control of the empire he helped build. Some things are not yet sorted, you see. While the paperwork is in progress, I'm not the only one with access to this office." That silver blue gaze locked on me, and the troubled emotions I saw there took my breath away. "One more person has the right to use it at any given time, for now."

"No." My whispered denial didn't stop the next thing coming from his mouth.

"My father." His deep voice was laced with reproach, but there was sadness there, too.

Chapter Twenty

It was the sadness that did me in, yet I had no idea why I wanted to argue with him on behalf of his father. I felt that I had to.

"Lies. Every word coming out of your mouth is a lie. I met your father, and he is a very nice, older gentleman. Why would he try to set me up?" My voice kept rising until I was practically shouting in his face. "What have I ever done to him? Or to you, if you want to get down to technicalities."

"You think all this was done because of you, malen'kaya ved'ma?" The smile curling his lips held no humor.

"I told you if you are going to insult me, do it in English so I can return the favor." Despite how rattled he appeared to be, the alpha smirked at me. "What does malele-whatever mean? You said it before once at the beach." Purposely butchering the pronunciation, I pinned him with a glare.

"Little witch," Dimitri told me simply, irrefutably shutting down everything I had geared up to throw in his face.

"Whatever." It wasn't easy to act like he hadn't flustered me. "My point is, stop trying to redirect the blame to your father. He has no reason to do all this to me. You, on the other hand …" I let my voice trail off, the implications obvious to anyone with half a brain. Well. Anyone but Dimitri, it turned out.

"And how did you come to that conclusion?" My reply was not fast enough, so he continued. "What motivation would I have to, as you say, 'set you up?'"

"Are you kidding me right now?" Gawking at him, I waved one of the daggers between us, but he didn't blink an eye at the sharp blade pointed in his direction. "You just got accepted in the MPO. What better way to show how powerful Dimitri Bell is but to bring a witch to their doorstep. Like a cat leaving birds' carcasses as an offering to its owner." The last part was a purposeful jab that made me preen inside when a feral growl rumbled deep in his chest.

It appeared the alpha didn't appreciate being reminded that he had a leash.

"I can see how this will appear to you as a set up." Dimitri surprised me. With a weary sigh, he rounded the desk, coming to stand in front of it before he leaned back, crossing one ankle over the other when he stretched out his long legs. "I assure you that the connection to you, at least on my part, was coincidental."

"Because your father is the one who did all this and threatened my life." Incredulity clear in the tone of my voice, I made sure my expression told him how ridiculous he sounded.

"I believe, Miss McCullough, his intentions with all this are a threat to my life, not yours."

The sound of a pin dropping could've been heard in the silent office.

"A lot of successful families bicker about inheriting money, estates, or in your case, empires. We are not in the middle ages anymore, so killing your father for a leather chair and an oak desk just wouldn't be right, Mr. Bell. There are many ways to settle disputes, and I'm sorry, but your father didn't look like a psycho killer to me." But doubt had already sprouted in the pit of my stomach, and his next words turned it into a full grown tree, branches and all.

"How many of those families have an alpha leading them, one whose son is taking over everything and has witch blood in him?"

It was my turn to pull back on my anger and look at everything in a new light. No matter how I turned it around, I couldn't deny the merit of what he'd shared.

"But why me?" I tucked the daggers in their sheaths. "Don't get me wrong, I'm really good at what I do, but I can think of at least a couple of others that could've done the job. For much cheaper, I might add, although I don't think money was an issue to begin with."

"The others might be good, but I am better." Some of his arrogance returned. "Had I known more about you before you walked inside my warded room, I would've prevented the theft and we wouldn't be in this mess now."

"Really?" Arching an eyebrow, I rolled my gaze over him. "You think you can stop me if I want to take something?"

"I know I can." It was stated as a fact, with all posturing lacking from the baritone rumbling in his chest. "The problem we have right now is much bigger than which one of us is better when it comes to magic."

"Actually, I don't see a problem that involves me here. This is between you and your father." Perking up at that, I even smiled at him. "I'm just the hired thief." Life seemed beautiful all of a sudden, but the shifter had to ruin it.

"Correct. You are just the thief who stole the magic from the two mages he sent to kill us and made them human." Folding his arms across his chest, he narrowed his impressive gaze on me. "I'd say you are free to live your life without consequence."

"It's your fault I had to do that," I spat at his reminder of what I'd done. "If you didn't just stand there like a lump, I wouldn't have had to resort to spells I've never used to save my life. Yours too." Rethinking the reason, I tucked the daggers away and pulled them right back out.

Dimitri cocked an eyebrow at me.

It happened so fast. One moment he was perched on the desk, and in the next, one of his hands was cradling the back of my head, the other wrapping around my waist and effectively pinning my arms until I was plastered to his chest. My breath caught from his nearness, and his wild scent, which was all male, when my nose filled with it.

"I saved your life, too." Goosebumps prickled my skin when his warm breath puffed over my cheeks. If I stretched just a little, our lips would've locked in a kiss. "The elementals knew how to block me from using my magic, but they were not prepared for you. I think we work well as a team, no?"

I was going to kiss him. Crazy or not, it was the only thought left in my head, and it was circling like a vulture. My soft curves molded to all the hard planes of his body, and I sagged in his hold. Eyes locked on his mouth, I parted my lips, and Dimitri tightened his grip on me. Swallowing thickly, I dragged my gaze excruciatingly slow to meet his, and that left me even more breathless than before. My heart rattled wildly in my chest, and his thumped in sync with it.

"Alaska." His deep voice, much lower than before, vibrated between us when he murmured my name in that thick accent of his.

My legs were like noodles, barely holding any of my weight.

I tilted my face up, bringing our lips closer.

The door burst open, and Char stormed in, her tote swinging from her shoulder and two round bottles full of a deadly potion clutched in her hands.

"Step away from her or I'll melt the skin off your handsome face," my friend snarled viciously at Dimitri.

We were still pressed together in an embrace, and all I could do was stare at her. The shifter had no intention of releasing his hold on me, it seemed. To her credit, Char didn't throw her potions without thinking. Her scowl flicked between us and turned into confusion.

"Oh ..." she mumbled and dropped her arms to her sides. "Oh! You were not trying to strangle her." With a sheepish, forced smile, she turned her back on us. "Don't mind me then. I'll just go wait outside until you kids are done. No rush, take your time. I'll stand guard in the hallway."

She was already pulling the door closed behind her when I snapped out of my stunned state. "Char." After I wiggled out of the stunned Dimitri's arms like an eel, I rushed after her, grabbing the door handle before it clicked shut. "It's not what you think."

"Mhm," was the reply from the other side of the slightly open, padded door we used as a tug-of-war.

"I swear it's not. Come back inside." My face was on fire and the chuckle that came from behind me nearly melted my skin. "Char, don't make me physically drag you in here."

"Fine." She released her hold, and the door swung with

me still clinging to it. I bounced off the opposite wall like a pinball and glared at her when she sashayed her butt in.

"Sorry, I really have bad timing." My friend, who was supposed to have *my* back, apologized to the wolf, although he still couldn't see her.

The audacity!

Chapter Twenty-One

"I knew that Dimitri had nothing to do with it." After repeating everything we discussed and turning her visible, I gawked at Char while the aforementioned wolf graced her with a friendly smile I'd never seen on his face until that moment.

"You wanted to wax all the fur off of his wolf." My reminder earned me a stare that promised bad things for my future if I lived long enough to have one.

"And the blonde?" Char mentioned Angela, and guilt drilled a hole in my chest. "Who was she?"

"His wife to be." I thumbed the air toward Dimitri.

"Another problem forced by my father that I will need to fix," the shifter rushed to assure my friend when she speared him with her disapproving glower. "If my suspicions are correct, Angela is the reason he hasn't reached out to collect the book. Why not take a rival pack down along with his son, if it's on the menu? Angela is the daughter of the alpha from our neighboring pack."

"Huh? He is too much into wedding planning, so he

forgot about his assassination attempts?" Although I hated the jealousy in my tone, I couldn't prevent voicing my bitterness. Char fought to keep the smile from emerging, but Dimitri's lips twitched at one corner.

Not one to go for just a pretty face, I couldn't understand my reaction to the shifter, especially after finding out about his engagement. I might be a witch, but I grew up reading and watching the story of *Little Red Riding Hood* often enough to know what happened to gullible, dumb little girls.

They got eaten by the big bad wolf, that was what.

A shiver slithered up and down my spine.

"... he doesn't understand that, if the truth comes out, he won't only be destroying me. Our entire empire, something he covets more than the life of his son, will go down with me," Dimitri grumbled, but I missed what he said before it.

"What exactly do you expect us to do?" From where I stood, there was a big fat zero on the possible things list that we could do.

"You could tell him that there was no book," the alpha suggested so casually I had to blink a few times in case I misheard him.

"I'm sorry, what?"

"You could say you tried but found nothing." He stopped my protests with a flick of a wrist. "That book is the only evidence he can use against me. After the attack on the beach, he already knows you are a witch, but that is something we can work with." Sincerity oozed out of him like honey. "I will protect you, Miss McCullough."

"Let me get this straight. You"—My finger poked at his chest since he stood close enough to touch—"will protect me"—The same finger jabbed at my own chest—"after you threatened me with exposing me to MPO? Did I hear that right?

"I simply needed the book and the name of who wanted it." Dimitri made a face as if he smelled something foul. It irked me that he pulled it off without looking like he made a grimace. "I wouldn't have done it."

"And I should trust you because …"

"Honor among thieves?" His arched eyebrow mocked me when he hit me with my own stones. Meanwhile, Char's head swiveled between us like she was watching a tennis match.

"No way, Jose." Strands of my hair slapped my cheeks from how hard my head shook. "Next. I'm not lying. If you knew anything about me, you'd know how ridiculous that plan is. I might be a thief, but a liar I'm not."

"She does have a point," Char chirped and shrugged when I looked at her angrily. "You suck at lying."

"It's the only way for all parties to walk away unharmed," Dimitri persisted.

"See, that's where you are wrong. It's the only way you and your psycho father walk away unharmed. I see a lot of harm coming my way with that plan." My feet shuffled toward the door. "We are wasting time here. I have bags to pack, scramming to do, and all that. Good luck with your wedding." My fingers wiggled in a goodbye, and I grabbed the doorknob.

"He will find you if you run." My blood turned to ice at the shifters even tone. "Here, I can protect you." I bristled at his boldness. Who the hell did he think he was?

Before I unloaded all my frustration on the alpha, Char spoke. "There is another way."

Dimitri and I perked up, and I shuffled to join them with a longing look aimed at the padded door.

Teeth rasping over her lower lip, my friend peered between us. "I can make a potion that will erase his memories of Alaska." The breath I sucked in was as loud as a bullet being fired inside the spacious office.

"You could do that?" As subtly as I could, I sent a pointed side-eye toward Dimitri. Char frowned at me, so I did it again. Why was she so heedless? I needed the alpha to forget all about me as much as I wanted his father to do the same. She should've said something long before about the existence of such a potion.

"If you make it, I'll make sure my father consumes it." Fast to agree, Dimitri straightened his shoulders.

"Making it is not a problem. Finding all the ingredients is a different story." After a moment, she pulled her tote open and rummaged through it. "I'll also need Allie's blood for it."

My whole body turned numb.

Even Dimitri jerked like she'd slapped him.

"Char, no." I snatched her arm and shook her to bring some sense to her. "You are not doing blood magic. Just no."

No one sane dabbled in that. Blood magic always took its toll, and I would never ask that from my worst enemy. The price paid was not worth the outcome.

"I appreciate the offer, Miss Mariatti, but I agree with your friend." Dimitri had some decency to back me up. "Protection is not a hardship on my part. We will sort this out without any harmful magic."

"Will you knock it off with the formalities, for goodness sake? We saw your bare ass in the middle of our store, along with half of Santa Monica. I'm sure it's okay to call us by our first names." There was no reason to go off like that, but I needed to take all the fear clawing at me out on someone, and Dimitri was the perfect target.

"Duly noted ... Allie." For a moment, I simply stared at that genuine curl on his full lips when he used my nickname in his accent. It did things to me that he had no right doing.

"It's Alaska to you. We are not that close." The shifter brought out the petulant child in me, and there was nothing I could do about it.

"Yet." Char coughed in her fist.

"What?"

"Nothing, I just need one thing to make this work. And stop trying to convince me not to make the potion. If there was a way to deal with this without spilling blood or getting into more trouble, we would've found it by now." Hitching the tote higher on her shoulder, she tapped her foot. I hated when she did that. "Let me remind you that I'm an adult woman. I can make my own decisions."

"Is there a way we can predict what the price will be for such a potion?" It showed how inept I was when it came to magic that Dimitri knew all the right questions to ask when I didn't. The excuse of being self-taught lingered in my mind, but it still irritated me.

"No. But it's fine. Erasing memory potions are among the less harmful ones to the person who brews them. If I leave now, I'd have one ready for you in a few hours, as long as I find the last ingredient."

"Can I help?" Ever the helpful, the shifter tensed as if already preparing to be Char's errand boy.

"I know who to ask." The way she said it told me the Druid picked the short end of the stick on that one. "I need to make a call. I'll be right back."

"We can't let her do this." I rounded on him as soon as my friend was gone and the door closed behind her. "I don't care if I have to kill your father, Char is not doing blood magic."

"I understand your concern, but I have to agree with her. And before you start waving your daggers at me, let me say one thing." He waited until I removed my hand from the hilt. "I'm confident that between us, we can figure out how to soften the impact on her."

"Look at you all all-knowing. If you understand blood magic so much, why don't you do it, huh?" Dimitri's flat stare was telling. Neither of us could brew a potion. Our powers didn't work that way, unfortunately.

"It'll be okay, Alaska." My power surged up when he took hold of my hand between both of his. The temperature dropped, and our breaths misted the air, but he acted like he didn't notice. "We will deal with one problem at a time. There must be a way to soften the impact."

"I'll never forgive myself if any harm comes to her."

"I won't allow it. You have my word."

Like an idiot, I believed him.

Chapter Twenty-Two

There was a track on the floor inside the shop, indicating where I'd paced for the few hours it took Char to brew the potion. Dimitri drove us in his fancy car to Burbank, where we picked up whatever Char needed from Damian. After that, she locked herself in the workshop. Leaning on the counter in front of the register, I stared at the small cut on my thumb where I sliced my skin with one of the daggers to give my friend a few drops of my blood.

That was when the waiting started.

Shards of glass and porcelain littered the floor, pieces we hadn't collected when we swept the mess from what felt like a lifetime ago. I was still tempted to repeat throwing candles at Dimitri when he showed his face. The alpha waited for our call so he could drag his father to Crystal Palace with a bogus story of picking up a gift for Angela. Apparently, they had a family dinner scheduled for later that evening. How very domesticated for the wolf.

Lost in my thoughts, I jumped when the bell above the door chimed, announcing a customer, but I could've sworn the sign was flipped to closed. However, I forgot to lock the door, it seemed. And since my day—or my last two weeks, for that matter—had not been bad enough, Jasmine pranced into my store, bringing a cloud of patchouli incense scent with her.

"Oh, you *are* open. Perfect." Her enthusiasm dampened when she noticed the mess on the floor. "I see you've had a little accident here."

"That's why the sign said closed," I deadpanned for nothing. She moved deeper inside, not halting until she was in front of me.

"I didn't come here for that." Leaning closer and bringing the odor of the incense in my face until I gagged, she whispered conspiratorially, although it was just the two of us in the whole store. "Was that Dimitri Bell I saw in your store the other day?" Leave it to Jasmine to know everyone who dared to visit our business, even on her days off work. "Naked?" Her eyes widened so much I was ready to catch them if they rolled out of their sockets.

I pressed the back of my hand to her forehead. "Are you sick?"

"What? No. Why? Do I look pale?" Her questions fired one after another, and she pressed both palms to her cheeks.

"You must've been hallucinating if you are seeing naked billionaires inside my store. I was checking if you still had a fever."

"You almost got me there." She chortled, smacking my arm.

Anxiety was a living thing inside my stomach, and I tried really hard not to panic or puke. One or the other. Jasmine's scent was not helping at all, and I wanted nothing more than for her to leave. The stars were not aligned in my favor, as usual, so I endured it with as little attitude as I could muster. Until Char popped out from the back and cleared her throat behind me.

"Jasmine." My friend sounded anything but happy to see the harpy. "I didn't expect you here."

Something in her tone made me glance at her over my shoulder, and I stiffened.

"Everything okay with the inventory?" I asked nonchalantly. In other words, did we have the potion.

"Yup. Mhm." My friend appeared nervous, and I found out why with her next comment. "I made the call for the pick-up." Luckily, I was pressed on the counter, or I would've crumbled on the floor when my knees buckled.

"Great, we can leave now." Urgency had me grabbing for the human to get her out of the store, but faster than she should've been able, Jasmine ducked away from my hand.

"I was just asking Alaska if that was Dimitri Bell I saw walking into your store the other day. Naked," she repeated the whole eye widening thing for Char.

"Don't I wish," my friend lied smoothly, giggling along with Jasmine. "He looked like him, right? I said the same to Allie, but she didn't believe me. The poor guy had someone steal his clothing and swimming trunks from one of the dressing rooms along the beach. We gave him a sarong so he could get to his car without being fined for indecent exposure."

"Damn," Jasmine gushed, folding her hands on her chest like in prayer." I could've sworn it was Bell."

"It wasn't." I took advantage of her dreamy state, grabbed her by the arm, and started dragging her to the door. "Sorry, but we must lock up and go."

"Oh, okay." Pretending like I hadn't tried to send her on her way since she'd walked in, the human pouted.

I nearly had her out on the sidewalk when the bell

chimed again, sending my stomach splattering at my feet. The doorway filled up with Dimitri Bell, and I could've sworn that Jasmine swoon dived, so I had to tighten my hold on her. My jaw clamped so hard I almost bit half of my tongue off. I was angry at the shifter more than anyone else. How on earth did he get to our store that fast?

"Good afternoon." Feigning indifference, I forced a smile at him when his father appeared behind his shoulder. "Are you here for the pick-up?"

Knowing what I knew about all the messed up things the older Bell had done, not just to me but to his own son, it was really hard to hold back everything I wanted to say. The older man smiled back at me cordially, which was worse than if he spat in my face.

"Yes, I received the call about ten minutes ago." Dimitri was all business. Not a trace of familiarity noticeable in the way he spoke. "Luckily we were nearby and I could pick it up without making another trip."

The insane plan we came up with in his office earlier that day was that he ordered an organic tea from our store especially made for Angela. At least as far as his father was concerned, they were buying a gift for his future daughter-in-law.

"Of course." Char rushed to greet them and ushered them inside. "I also made a couple of samples from the tea so you can try it. That way, you'll know what you'll be giving your loved one."

Bile burned the roof of my mouth, but I swallowed it down.

Head ducked low so the older man couldn't see the hatred in my eyes, I propelled the still gawking Jasmine forward. To my horror, the human dug her heels in, refusing to budge. I had half a mind to smack her with a spell that would make all the hair from her head fall out.

"I want to try the tea, as well." Protesting loudly, she yanked her arm out of my grip. "I might order some, too." Unless I wanted to create drama, I had no choice but to stand back.

"Why of course, dear." Dimitri's father turned toward the human, all smiles and pleasantness and no sign of the psycho lurking within. "You can have mine, if that is okay?" He peered at me beseechingly like I was the one denying Jasmine her damn tea. "I'm sure Angela will be happy to make me a cup when we get there." That last part was aimed at Dimitri.

I wanted to cry, scream, or start breaking everything in the store. This could not be happening. If Char paid a price for doing blood magic only so Jasmine could hang around Dimitri Bell and mess up our plans, I was going to kill the human, consequences be damned.

"Oh, nonsense." Char waved her hand in dismissal and pulled me from my murderous thoughts. "I made enough for everyone. We never sell anything that does not meet our high standards. Sampling is the best way to perfecting a product."

My sigh came all the way from my toes.

"Allie, can you help me please? We will be right back," my friend told the three people in our store, and without waiting for a reply, she nudged me toward the door behind the counter.

I didn't need to be told twice, and bolted like my behind was on fire.

"I'm going to kill her." I seethed in the back. "I swear I will give her hemorrhoids, along with making her hair fall out."

"You're funny." Cool as a cucumber, Char busied herself with pouring tea I didn't know she made into small shot glasses. "This actually turned out better than planned." We both avoided mentioning the tremor in her hands or the quaver in her voice. "I also called Damian, just in case. He should be here any moment."

"How is Jasmine being here a good thing?"

"It won't look suspicious if random people drink *the tea.*" She made air quotes with her fingers. "He knows something is up, I can feel it."

"This was a dumb idea." Dutifully, I held the tray where she placed the small glasses filled to the brim. "So we are all drinking a memory-erasing potion? Am I going to forget myself too?" although Jasmine forgetting all about me sounded heavenly.

"Nope." Without any further explanation, she pointed at the glass closest to me. "You'll take that one."

"Okay." Grumbling, I followed her back to the front of the store.

I almost spilled everything when we found Jasmine draped over Dimitri like a chinchilla coat. The human was squeezing his bicep like a stress ball, and my vision turned red. To his credit, the shifter made a valid effort to pry her roaming fingers off him with no avail. Internally, I chanted *"Don't kill the human, don't kill the human,"* while the older man watched me like the cat that ate the canary.

"Time to test the tea." Char clapped her hands just as I placed the tray on the counter, and that removed Jasmine from Dimitri.

I waited while she handed one glass to the human, one to Dimitri, and reached a third toward the older Bell. His fingers brushed the glass when I picked mine up, and the liquid just about tipped over when, instead of taking what Char offered him, he snatched mine from my hand.

"Thank you, dear." The genial smile on his face was a tad too sweet and forced for my liking.

"You're welcome." The words were pushed through my teeth. Panic formed dark spots at the corners of my vision.

We messed it up. Instead of the old man, it would be me who forgot myself. Numbly, I felt another glass being pressed in my hand, and I tipped it to my lips, unseeing. Jasmine gushed about fruity flavors and the universe knew what else, but it was all distant noise coming from afar. The potion had a tang to it that I actually liked, and for a moment, I wondered if the flavor was that way because of my blood.

"Are you alright, Miss?" a deep voice pulled me to the present, and I blinked up at Dimitri.

"Yes, I'm fine." I still remembered who I was, so the potion didn't work, obviously. Disappointment smacked me like a brick until I glanced at the alpha's father.

The old man looked confused.

"Dimitri." His father cleared his throat, seeming lost as he turned to look this way or that. "I think we should go, or we will be late." His eyes mostly stayed on me, full of puzzlement.

My heart skipped a beat when Dimitri gave my forearm a reassuring, as well as comforting, squeeze. Jasmine stared daggers at me from behind him.

"I absolutely love the tea. Thank you." The shifter turned to Char. "The cost was fully covered with my payment?"

"Yes, fully paid." My friend beamed at him and pulled out a gift bag from under the counter, which she placed in his hand. "If you need more of it, just call. A day or so in advance if possible, in case we are missing some of the ingredients." A ton of hidden meaning was packed in her conversational tone.

"Have a good day." Gift bag tucked into the inside pocket of his suit jacket, Dimitri and his father left, taking the tension with them. His silver blue gaze flicked to me a time or two, but I was too numb to return it.

The bell chimed as they left.

"It wasn't Dimitri Bell." Jasmine glowered at us with both hands slapped on her hips. "I know what I saw."

"If anyone mentions Dimitri Bell in the next ten years around me, I swear I'm going to lose it." Jasmine had some self-preservation, so she took a step away from me when I hissed at her.

"It worked." There was wonder and pride in Char's whisper, so I turned to face my friend with my heart thumping in my throat. She grinned so wide all her teeth were showing. "It worked, Allie."

"It was nice. I'd give you that," the human mumbled, and we both ignored her.

"How very anticlimactic." Rattled by the whole thing, I wanted to laugh in relief. I couldn't believe it was over and no more killers would be nipping on my heels.

For the umpteenth time, a chime bounced around the nearly empty store, and I turned toward the door expecting to find Jasmine gone. Instead, the human stood in the same spot, eyeing us warily while a Druid graced us with his presence.

"Damian, hi." Smiling, I glanced from him to my friend so I wouldn't miss her blush.

"Allie, Char, how are you ladies?" He sounded very happy to see us, but I couldn't breathe.

"I'm sorry." Char frowned slightly. "Do we know each other?"

Damian froze in his tracks, and dread filled me.

Char didn't remember who the Druid was, and my heart hurt for my friend. I never lied to myself so I knew the potion we gave the older man was a bandaid not a permanent cure. When it wore off fresh hell would be unleashed on my life.

Dimitri Bell was going to wish it was his father gunning for him after all that.

I was going to kill the damn wolf.

Next in the Honor Among Thieves series

vinci-books.com/stolenoath

Witches and shifters never mix well.

Alaska never meant to get tangled in a shifter's family feud, but Dimitri's legacy holds secrets—and deadly consequences. With a stolen vow binding them and a father willing to erase his son, Alaska must do the impossible: steal back her freedom. If only magic were that simple.

Turn the page for a free preview…

Stolen Oath: Chapter One

The cheery chime of the bell above the door registered at the back of my subconscious like an annoyingly persistent buzzing of a mosquito. It echoed perpetually behind my eyeballs to the point of madness. Being agitated made me twitchy and unreasonable at the best of times, so you could imagine my state of mind that morning.

A jerk was an understatement of what I was.

My brain was mush from the lack of sleep in the last couple of weeks, and naturally, any type of noise didn't help much in my attempts to stay sane or civil. I wanted to snarl and snap at anyone who walked into the store just to make sure every single person was as miserable as I was.

Adulting at its finest, I had no doubt.

The truth of the matter is, I wanted to be numb and to be grateful for the numbness; Because then I wouldn't have to acknowledge the crushing weight of my guilt while suffocating under it. I neither knew, nor cared, I just wanted the weight of the elephant sitting on my chest gone.

Thinking myself invincible, I stole a magic book full of

ancestral spells—that was not supposed to exist, mind you—from none other than Dimitri Bell, alpha of the Southern California pack and newest member of the MPO.

My ego, as I always feared, would be my downfall.

The fact that it was Dimitri's father who hired me sent all of us into an impossible situation between a rock and a hard place. Instead of coming up with a solid plan, the old alpha pushed us into a corner where we acted rashly and defensively, and because of that, my best friend dabbled in blood magic and potions that were best left alone for goodness sake. As a result, she lost part of herself in the process.

I wanted to shriek and rage until I destroyed myself and there was nothing left of me.

I failed Char, I failed Dimitri, and I failed myself too. And for what?

Nothing. That's what.

Others were paying for my mistakes.

Char was paying for them more than anyone else, which was the core of my problem if I is being honest.

A ray of sunshine was caught in a slow, sensual dance with one of the crystals, casting bursts of colors across the floor like a liquid fire snaking over the vinyl before it bounced up and glittered over the displayed candles and statues. The coward that I am, I watched it with a desperation of a man dying from thirst seeing a fat, juicy droplet of water. It was going great too until someone cleared their throat close enough that I could smell the tuna this person has eaten in the last hour or so for breakfast.

"Welcome to the Crystal Palace," I mumbled dully and dragged my eyes from the floor to the person in front of the counter. "How can I help you?"

"Namaste." The young woman smiled demurely at me before bowing her head in a practiced swan move she must've done at least a thousand times in front of a mirror. How I knew? It was either practiced or she was a time traveler from the Middle Ages where she curtsied and bowed to royalties and suitors on a daily basis. She was all elegance and grace that was faker than the three-inch caterpillar lashes the lady checking out the incense to our right had glued to her poor eyelids.

I glanced briefly at the paperweight sitting inconspicuously next to the register and felt guilty about it immediately. Guilty that I caught myself eyeing it, and for wanting to throw it at swan lake in front of me. Instead of doing what I wanted to do, I forced a smile and jerked my head in a nod.

"Namaste to you too. What can I do for you?"

"I was hoping to find one of the love candles you normally have displayed in that corner." Her arm lifted gracefully as she pointed toward the left corner of the store where the specialty candles were lined up like soldiers. An empty space gapped in the spot where a red love candle usually sat.

"I'm sorry, I didn't notice we sold the last one. I can make one for you but you'll have to come back and pick it up later this afternoon or tomorrow. Whatever works for you, as long as you leave a deposit." My hand was already reaching for the register so I can charge her and get her away from me as fast as I could, but it wasn't written in the stars it seemed.

"But I need it now." With a sharp, reprimanding voice, she folded her arms over her chest and my hand froze a hairsbreadth away from the register. "Not later this afternoon and not tomorrow, that's for sure. Now, sister." The last part was said almost mockingly. I knew I should've stayed home and avoided any interaction.

Something primal and scary perked up inside of me at her tone, and like the predator that I was, my head cocked to the side on its own and my vision sharpened on her features. For the first time, I noticed the tiny beads of sweat around her hairline and on her upper lip, which was trembling slightly despite her holier-than-thou attitude.

My instincts were screaming at me that something was off about the lady.

"And why is that, sister?" Not even my sneer made her pay attention that she was treading on dangerous grounds. "What's so important that can't wait a few hours? We don't sell generic, mass-market candles. Each is made here in the shop."

"You don't understand and I don't expect you to, but I can't stand a second longer with her having those painted claws all over him. He needs to come back to where he belongs. With me. Now, not this afternoon or tomorrow." With each word she was becoming more agitated and she tapped her forefinger on the counter to make her point.

"You're looking for a candle to return a lost lover?" My eyes narrowed suspiciously on her.

It wasn't my place to question customers. For my morals' sake, I wanted to occasionally, maybe, but not if I wanted to run a successful business. After all, I prided myself that I did something good with the candles, even when everything else in my life was pushing the limits of ethical grounds. Yet memories of Dimitri and the desperation in his eyes when he talked about his obligations along with placating his father in hopes to keep him away from destroying his life raked my insides with razor blades. The fact that I would've felt better if the handsome alpha was unattached had nothing to do with it. I almost convinced myself of that too.

Almost.

"We were happy." A tear glistened in her right eye that rolled down her cheek and I tracked every twitch of her muscles like a hawk. "I was his world until she came along and convinced him they were soulmates. She must've given him a potion or something. I need him back."

"Because he is your soulmate? Not hers?"

The shop disappeared into a blurry fog when I focused solely on her, and in slow motion I watched her chest expand as she took a deep breath while another tear rolled down her face. My problem was, the sadness which usually pulled at my heartstrings as customers asked for my aid was missing from her hooded gaze. Instead, rage lurked in her irises, calling to the magic inside my veins to come to the surface and burn everything in my path. My intuition reacted to her deceit immediately.

"Yes." The young woman lifted her hand and casually tucked a strand of strawberry blonde hair behind her ear. The bracelets on her forearm slid down and tinkled in the silence that hummed in my ears. "Mine. Not hers."

And there it was, that cunning glint in her eyes. If I wasn't watching her as closely as I was, I would've missed it.

"You don't need a love candle for that." Leaning back casually so she doesn't notice I was trying to distance myself from whatever was off with her, I gave her a practiced smile. "I have something better. Wait right here."

Her face cleared and the sadness she faked horribly was replaced by triumph, instantly.

Should I have kept my nose out of her business? Probably.

Was it my job to teach her a lesson? Absolutely not.

Was I going to stick my nose in her business and teach

her a lesson she will never forget nonetheless? Hell yeah, I was.

You don't get to play with people's lives and get away with it.

Not if I can help it.

My flats whispered over the tiled floor as I rushed to the back of the store where my candles waited their turn to be displayed. Not wasting time, in case I changed my mind, I practically snatched the multicolored one from the top of the box it was perched on. The patterned texture of the purple wax rasped over my fingers almost in a loving caress when the traces of my magic I'd left in it reacted to my presence. I glanced down at it, checking that the black and red inside layers were a perfect thickness out of habit and my thumb rubbed the black tourmaline stone pressed on the outside layer at the center, making sure it won't wobble or dislodge. It wont do any good if the stone is not on the candle when it does the reverse spell it was meant to do.

The curtain grazed the exposed skin on my back where the tank top didn't cover it when I returned to the front of the store and I shivered. Another chill crawled up my spine at the voracious look the woman had while her eyes were glued to my hand holding the beautiful candle.

A small tug curled one side of my mouth at her expression.

"What is it for?" she breathed out in anticipation, already reaching outward with her greedy fingers so she can touch the candle.

"This one will restore everything the way it was," I said proudly and truthfully. "No need for rituals, full moon, or chanting. Just go home, light it up, and say thank you."

Without looking away from it, she waved her credit card at me and snatched the candle hard enough to leave wax under my fingernails because I didn't release it fast enough. A sensation I couldn't name poked its head up inside me but I pushed it away. There were more important things to deal with than horrible humans like the one impatiently waiting on me to finish the transaction.

So engrossed in my thoughts, I didn't notice we were not alone at the register anymore. My heart skipped a beat when I lifted my head to hand her her card with the receipt and a storm blue gaze captured mine like a snare.

"Thank you so much, sister." The woman yanked her card from my fingers but I couldn't look at her if I tried. Instead, I blinked at the person standing behind her. "Namaste," she spat at me, and then she was gone.

"Let me guess, that was not a love candle?" Dimitri glided closer and casually leaned on the counter. The scent of citrus and musk tickled my nose and my belly tightened in reaction to his nearness sending butterflies into a frenzy in my lower belly.

"How long were you standing there?" I had to clear my throat because I sounded breathless to the point of embarrassment and ducked my head so I could hide my face with my hair.

"Long enough to know that poor guy is not her soulmate?" He murmured the statement more like a question and his eyebrow cocked up as he side-eyed me. Transixed I peaked at him through the strands of hair covering half of my face. "Or that the candle she bought is not a love candle." A small smile played on his lips. He spoke as if he was reprimanding me, yet he never said anything of the sort, remaining quiet and watching the woman walk out of the store with the candle.

"You trust my judgment?" It's not like I wanted his

approval or anything, but my tone suggested that I very much did.

"To a point, yes. I trust this too." He tapped his nose with his forefinger and a braided, leather cord dangled from his wrist that hit me like a punch to the gut. "I can smell a lie from a mile away." Wolves gave each other promised leather cords to wear on their wrists when they were engaged. My jaw clenched tight enough to grind my molars and of course the alpha didn't miss my reaction. I was grateful he chose to let it slide since I've already embarrassed myself in front of him more times than I'd like to count. "What does the candle do?" He searched my face while I composed myself to answer him without squeaking like a five-year-old.

"It restores the balance. Everything she has done to tweak anyone's mind or actions, or any negative energy she sent out will return to her... tenfold." My shoulder twitched in a half shrug like it was nothing, though it was anything but. "I hope she shopped elsewhere for anything she's done until today. It'll be horrible to know I've unintentionally helped her do bad things to people if she has been buying her tools in my store."

"Vicious, Miss McCullough." The grin brightened his face so much it made it look almost boyish.

Yet there was nothing boyish at all about Dimitri Bell.

"I don't like it when someone tries to mess with people and their free will." My tone was sharp and short, maybe even a tid bit louder than intended, I found myself defensive for some silly reason. "People should not be forced to do anything they choose not to do. Not if I can help it, anyway." *You shouldn't do anything against your will either,* - but that part I kept to myself.

Dimitri sharpened his gaze on me and stayed silent long

enough to make me want to squirm where I stood. I resisted with everything in me and watched fascinated as something clicked behind his stormy irises as he either made a decision or I confirmed something for him. Whatever it was, I truly believe that very moment, for better or for worse, sealed both our fates.

"I hope you hold that word. As a matter of fact, I'm counting on it, Allie." He said my nickname with a barely there rasp to his tone, which made me tremble visibly. To add insult to injury, he winked after seeing the effect he had on me.

In answer, my snort had no humor in it, yet he threw his head back and laughed as if I had told him the funniest joke ever.

I did say he was a jerk, didn't I?

Stolen Oath: Chapter Two

"Why are you here again?" Pretending I was busy, and failing miserably, I kept rearranging the crystals over and over so I don't have to maintain eye contact with Dimitri. Or keep thinking about the woman and her lies.

His wolf unnerved me on the best of days. Why was he in my store? Why?

"I thought friends visit each other?" Reaching over my shoulder and standing too close for comfort, he nudged a crustal to the right unnecessarily. My attempt to get away from him was unsuccessful. He just followed leisurely behind me no matter where I went. "Was I wrong in my assumption? You look upset that I am here. Why?"

That thick accent of his was to blame for my knees being wobbly. He knew exactly what he was doing and stupidly, I did nothing to stop him. I didn't smack his hand when his fingers grazed my arm as he stepped back either. I simply shivered like a fool. Witch or not, I was a woman, damn it.

I was weak when it came to Dimitri Bell.

"We're friends now?" My mouth snapped shut as soon as the words were out. It shouldn't have sounded like a challenge but it did. His low chuckle confirmed my stupidity.

"What would you like us to be if not friends, Miss McCullough?" Dimitri slid close enough that I could feel the heat of his body on my skin. Without a conscious thought, my body leaned back to be closer to him before I became aware of my actions. When I did become aware of what I was doing I jerked away from him as if electricted.

"We should ask your fiancée," I ground out between my teeth. "I'm sure she would love to tell us the answer."

A statue rattled on a shelf nearby, snapping me out of the fog my brain dived into around the alpha. The lady who bumped it grimaced while her face reddened, as if she felt bad for getting my attention while eavesdropping on our conversation. One look around and I realized that the store had filled up while I was too busy swooning at Dimitri like a school girl, and everyone was watching us, watching him to be exact, while pretending they were busy perusing the merchandize. It was like a bucket of cold water being dumped over my head. Feeling sick to my stomach from my beheivor I straightened my shoulders, jutting my chin out stubburnly. I was the master of my emotions not the other way around.

Dimitri had the same effect on any breathing creature. Male or female alike.

He was a juicy steak in the center of a group of hungry beasts.

"I'm an idiot." Angrily smacking his hand away from where he was curling a strand of my hair around his finger, I practically ran for the register. Salvation waited for me as soon as I placed the glass display between us, at least, I hoped that it would. "I don't want us to be anything, Mr. Bell. I do, however, want you to leave my store, if you don't mind. I have things to do instead of playing these games with you."

"I'm not sure how it's good for business to chase away customers." Goddess help me, unperturbed, he stalked me inside my own store. The nerve of this guy.

"You're a customer now?" I tripped while diving behind the register and whacked my elbow on the edge of the counter. My eyes rolled to the back of my head from the stabbing pain that radiated up and down my arm, numbing it all the way to my shoulder. I thought I heard a tooth crack from how hard I clenched my jaw so I wouldn't yelp.

"Of course, I'm a customer," Dimitri said simply and, without permission, reached over the counter, pulled my arm across it, and leaned over to inspect the red, rapidly swelling spot marking my injury. "Supporting local, small businesses is very important for the economy."

Lips parted, I gawked at the top of his head while he gently lifted my arm and soothed my pain by blowing air on it. Gripping the counter in a white-knuckled desperation prevented my fingers from sinking into his hair. My chest tightened because the simple act overwhelmed me with an emotion I didn't dare name. Goose bumps puckered along my skin from the heat that radiated from his pursed lips.

I was in so much trouble.

"How very benevolent of you." My barely above a whisper comment made him glance up at me and my heart skipped a beat from his penetrating stare. "But honestly, I thought we agreed to meet up only when necessary to avoid complications. We can't afford to mess up and trigger some of your father's memories. Not when Char already paid a steep price for it. We're not ready to face him or anyone else that might be involved until we find out more about this whole thing."

"You will forgive me, Alaska, but I cannot sit and pretend like everything is normal, or whatever passes for normal these days for any of us. We know there is more to the situation than just my father wanting to remove me from a position of power or to expose you for... well, you know." Ignoring the hungry looks the women were throwing his way, he rubbed his thumb over the sore spot on my arm, slightly frowning at it, while I frantically searched the store to make sure no one could hear him. The fear for my life made me forget he was touching me like he had every right to do so. I needn't worry though, because he seemed like he was talking more to himself than me and I just happened to be near enough to hear him. "If that was the endgame, he could've gotten me killed or you captured. I need to do something. Anything."

"He can try to catch me anytime he wants." My arrogant snort told him exactly what I thought the chances of anyone catching me were. Well, anyone but Dimitri. As far as I knew, there were no other witches in LA. "Let's hope he holds his breath for it, it might save us all a lot of trouble if he kicks the bucket from oxygen deprivation, but it's not from lack of trying to kill you on his part that you are still alive, wolf. Did you forget the mages?" A shiver worked its way up my body when the memory of being underwater while the ocean raged around me squeezed me in its grip.

It also brought another thing to the forefront of my mind. The fact that in my panic, while thinking we were about to die, I stole magic from the elementals and rendered them human, petrified me.

"No." Lifting his gaze to mine, he held me suspended in a space where the oxygen was thinning with each beat of my heart. "How can I forget that you saved my life, *lyubimyy milyy*."

"Yeah..." Breathless and bothered like every time he would say something in Russian and I had no doubt it was another endearment as was his style, I shook my head to clear it. "I'm dumb like that." My mind told me to take a step back and put more distance between us but I couldn't move to save my life. My feet were glued to the floor.

"And here I thought you cared." He clicked his tongue in faked disappointment before removing his hand from my injured elbow, taking away with him the tantalizing scent that was clouding my mind, and straightening to his full height. Without the physical connection, I finally felt like I could breathe again, though I hated that I missed his touch almost immediately.

"What does it mean?" I asked, despite the fact I knew it was a bad idea. "What you just called me."

He simply smiled, not giving me an answer.

"There was an unexpected development recently in regards to our arrangement. I was hoping to speak with you,"—the shifter looked around the store for the first time and appeared surprised to see it was almost packed. Little did he know, it had nothing to do with the merchandise I was selling and everything to do with the handsome male in front of me—"privately. Let me take you to lunch."

"You could've just called if you wanted to ask me to lunch," I grumbled petulantly, glancing pointedly at the phone perched close to the register in a not so subtle way of telling him *don't you dare call my cell phone*. That'd be a little too familiar for my peace of mind. "Sorry, but it's too early for lunch, plus I'm alone this morning. I can't go anywhere until Char comes to work."

There. That was a good excuse to avoid temptation.

"Speaking of which..." Dimitri smiled as he watched the front door suddenly and expectantly.

The bell above the door rattled a second later, filling the space with the annoyingly cheery chime. Damn shifters and their supernatural hearing. I bet he heard my best friend walking this way from a mile away. The widening of his grin when he looked back at me confirmed it while I glared daggers at his smug face.

"Brunch then." He had the gall to wink, again.

"You can bow now, peasant, your goddess is here." Char swooped in with a grace of a falcon, zeroing in on me from across the store, and saved Dimitri from a nasty curse. I had a couple of them circling in my mind that would've made him regret being all cocky.

Not that I would've cursed him for real. It was just a better alternative to think about that than imagining all the ways I would've loved to climb him like a tree.

A few chuckles met Char's theatrical entrance, the regulars being familiar with our typical antics, and they either waved at her or simply sent her kisses. Everyone loved Char. The moment my bestie locked eyes with me though, I knew something was wrong and my back stiffened.

"I hold your life in my hand." To hide her emotions, she made a show of lifting the paper tray full of coffee cups like it was the holy grail, but I could read the uneasiness she felt in every muscle of her body.

Unsure of what was going on I played along, grabbing at the air in the direction of the coffee she bought for us. "Gimme. I could kiss you right now for bringing a couple of extra cups."

"Pfft, who in their right mind would be happy with just one cup? I can tease men by batting my eyelashes without giving them my phone number. I don't have a death wish to tease a woman with just one cup of coffee." Char proceeded to bat her lashes at Dimitri who in turn, snickered.

"Miss Marietti, it is a pleasure to see you again." Dimitri took hold of Char's shoulders in his hands and kissed her once on each cheek.

"Dimitri!" You'd think the two of them were best friends since birth with how my best friend beamed at him. I was biting the inside of my cheek so I that couldn't tell them where to shove it. They'd been acting like this the last week or so. "*Kak tvoy osel?*" she spoke slowly and deliberately in his mother tongue, vibrating from excitement.

Char can speak Russian? Say what now?

Dimitri threw his had back and laughed heartedly.

"Oh, dear goddess." Char slapped her free hand over her mouth and giggled. "Please tell me I didn't insult your mother?"

I gawked at them.

"You did not." Shoulders still shaking from laughter, he took the tray of coffee cups from her hand and placed it on the counter. "And to answer your question, if I had a donkey, I assure you it would be doing amazingly well. I, on the other hand, am very hungry, but Miss McCullough here refuses to take me to lunch."

"I asked how your donkey is doing?" Char shook her head, laughing along with him. "This will teach me to blindly trust the internet." Curls bouncing, she turned to me, with a raised brow and a smirk on her beautiful face. "And you, Missy? Why are you keeping the wolf hungry? You hoping he will give up on food and gobble you up?"

I felt the heat on my face bloom like a cloud around my head. Dimitri was snickering along with her but his smoldering gaze added a few extra degrees to the temperature of my reddening cheeks. It was up to me to put a stop to their nonsense.

"What's wrong?" I searched Char's face, ignoring the alpha who was watching me as if he was trying to memorize my features. A maddening hum was thudding in my ears as my heart sped up from his attention.

Glancing left and right to assure no one was near, my best friend leaned in toward me. "I think someone has been following me all morning. That's why it took me so long to get here. I tried to lose whoever it was."

All humor forgotten, Dimitri and I sobered up immediately. My skin prickled from the power that the alpha unleashed, warning anything supernatural within a ten-mile radius that this was his territory and that he will protect it at all costs.

I've heard stories about alphas of his caliber, I'd just never experienced it at that level. He was terrifying in that moment as much as he was exuberant. Primal.

"Mages?" Keeping my tone low, I reached under the counter and pulled out the two kukri knives I stashed there for emergency situations after the vampire attack in our apartment not long ago. Their weight in my palms grounded me to the present more than anything else could've.

"I'm not sure." Char's dark eyes sparkled with anger as she leaned in even closer. "Humans were everywhere this morning so I couldn't do anything about it, but if the stalkers step foot in here, it's game on." Pulling away from me with a wicked and humorless smile, she patted her purse. "I'm going to split them up."

A shiver worked its way up my spine. I loved her to pieces but she scared the crap out of me sometimes.

Suddenly, the bell above the door rattled, filling the store with a jolly peal. All three of our heads snapped toward the entrance, our bodies tensed up and ready to go.

"It's them," Char breathed out.

Grab your copy...
vinci-books.com/stolenoath

About the Author

Maya Daniels, USA Today Bestselling and multi-award-winning supernatural suspense author, is a fun-loving woman with many talents.

She traveled the world, gaining life experiences that helped her career as an investigative journalist, as well as her storytelling. Maya writes compelling tales of magic, mythical creatures, loyalty, and life-changing friendships with snarky female characters—much like herself.

Her travels have taken her to Europe, Africa, Asia, Australia, and America. Born with her feet in motion, she currently resides in Ohio, spinning her next epic story that you will not want to put down.

Her biggest 'sins' are her love of chocolate and coffee—through an IV drip! One to never sit still, Maya practices Reiki healing, different types of martial arts, reads about the arcane, talks to furry creatures more than humans, picks up a sledgehammer for home improvement, and travels with her fated mate, seeking her own adventures.

www.ingramcontent.com/pod-product-compliance
Ingram Content Group UK Ltd.
Pitfield, Milton Keynes, MK11 3LW, UK
UKHW040035130426
469799UK00003B/119